STONE COLD

A Jesse Stone novel

Robert B Parker

STONE COLD

A Jesse Stone novel

NO EXIT PRESS

This edition published in 2004 by No Exit Press
18 Coleswood Road, Harpenden, Herts, AL5 1EQ

www.noexit.co.uk

First published in the UK by John Murray (Publishers) Ltd

A CIP catalogue record for this book is available from the British Library.

ISBN 1-84243-116-1 Stone Cold

2 4 6 8 10 9 7 5 3 1

FOR JOAN:

everything started to hum

STONE COLD

1

...he murder, they made love in front of a video cam-
...en it was over, her mouth was bruised. He had long
...across his back. They lay side by side on their
... ...ing for breath.
... ...e said, his voice hoarse.
of ... ...whispered.
... ...nto the compass of his left arm and rested her
bell ... ...s chest. They lay silently for a while, not
... ...for oxygen.
... ...e said.
... ...," she said.
en he ... ...own against the top of her head where it

lay on his chest. Her hair smelled of verbena. In time their breathing settled.

"Let's play the video," she whispered.

"Let's," he said.

The camera stood beside the bed on a tripod. He got up, took the tape from it, put it in the VCR, got back into bed, and picked up the remote from the night table. She moved back into the circle of his arm, her head back on his chest.

"Show time," he said, and clicked the remote.

They watched.

"My God," she said. "Look at me."

"I love how you're looking right into the camera," he said.

They watched quietly for a little while.

"Whoa," she said. "What are you doing to me there?"

"Nothing you don't like," he said.

When the tape was over he rewound it.

"You want to watch again?" he said.

She was drawing tiny circles on his chest with her left forefinger.

"Yes."

He started the tape again.

"You know what I loved," she said. "I loved the range expression on his face."

"Yes," he said, "that was great. First it's like, *what the is this?*"

"And then like, *are you serious?*"

"And then, *omigod!*"

"That's the best," she said. "The way he looked wl

knew we were going to kill him. I've never seen a look like that."

"Yes," he said. "That was pretty good."

"I wish we could have made it last longer," she said.

He shrugged.

"My bad," she said. "I got so excited. I shot too soon."

"I've been known to do that," he said.

"Well, aren't you Mr. Dirty Mouth," she said.

They both laughed.

"We'll get better at it," he said.

She was now rubbing the slow circles on his chest with her full palm, looking at the videotape.

"Ohhh," she said. "Look at me! Look at me!"

He laughed softly. She moved her hand down his stomach.

"What's happening here?" she said.

He laughed again.

"Ohh," she said. "Good news."

She turned her body hard against him and put her face up.

"Be careful," she murmured. "My mouth is sore."

They made love again while the image of their previous lovemaking moved unseen on the television screen, and the sounds of that mingled with the sounds they were making now.

2

It was just after dawn. Low tide. Several herring gulls hopped on the beach, their heads cocking one way then another, their flat black eyes looking at the corpse. Jesse Stone, with the blue light flashing, pulled into the public beach parking lot at the end of the causeway from Paradise Neck, parked behind the Paradise Police cruiser that was already there, and got out of his car. It was mid November and cold. Jesse closed the snaps on his Paradise Men's Softball League jacket and walked to the beach, where Suitcase Simpson, holding a big Mag flashlight, stood looking down at the body.

"Guy's been shot, Jesse," he said.

Jesse stood beside Simpson and looked down at the body.

"Who found him?"

"Me. I'm on eleven to seven and I pulled in here to, ah, take a leak, you know, and the headlights picked him up."

Simpson was a big shapeless red-cheeked kid who'd played tackle in high school. His real name was Luther but everyone called him Suitcase after the ballplayer.

"Peter Perkins coming?"

"Anthony's on the night desk," Simpson said. "He told me he'd call him soon as he called you."

"Okay, gimme the flashlight. Then go pull your cruiser across the entrance to the parking lot and call in. When Molly comes on I want Anthony down here and everybody else she can wrangle. I want the area secured."

Simpson hesitated, still looking down.

"It's a murder, isn't it, Jesse?"

"Probably," Jesse said. "Gimme the light."

Simpson handed the flashlight to Jesse and went to his cruiser. Jesse squatted on his heels and studied the corpse. It had been a young white man, maybe thirty-five. His mouth was open. There was sand in it. He wore a maroon velour warm-up suit, which was soaking wet. There were two small holes in the wet fabric. One on the left side of the chest. One on the right. Jesse turned the head slightly. There was sand in his ear. Jesse swept the flashlight slowly around the body. He saw nothing but the normal debris of a normal beach: a tangle of seaweed scraps, a piece of salt-bleached driftwood, an empty crab shell.

Simpson walked back across the parking lot. Behind him the blue light on his patrol car revolved silently.

"Perkins is on the way," he said. "And Arthur Angstrom. Anthony called Molly. She's coming in early. Anthony'll be down as soon as she gets there."

Jesse nodded, still looking at the crime scene.

He said, "What time is it, Suit?"

"Six-fifteen."

"And it's dead low tide," Jesse said. "So high was around midnight."

A siren sounded in the distance.

"You think he was washed up here?" Simpson said.

"Body that's been in the ocean and washed up on shore doesn't look like this," Jesse said.

"More beat up," Simpson said.

Jesse nodded.

"He's got some marks on his face," Simpson said.

"That would probably be the gulls," Jesse said.

"I coulda lived without knowing that," Simpson said.

Jesse moved the right arm of the corpse. "Still in rigor," he said.

"Which means?"

"Rigor usually passes in twenty-four hours," Jesse said.

"So he was killed since yesterday morning."

"More or less. Cold water might change the timing a little."

A Paradise patrol car pulled in beside Simpson's, adding its blue light to his. Peter Perkins got out and walked toward them. He was carrying a black leather satchel.

"Anthony says you got a murder?" Perkins said.

"You're the crime-scene guy," Jesse said. "But there's two bullet holes in his chest."

"That would be a clue," Perkins said.

He put the satchel on the sand and squatted beside Jesse to look at the corpse.

"I figure he was probably shot here, sometime before midnight," Jesse said, "when the tide was still coming in. There's the high water line. The tide reached high about midnight and soaked him, maybe rolled him around a little, and left him here when it receded."

"If you're right," Perkins said, "it probably washed away pretty much any evidence might be lying around."

"We'll close the beach," Jesse said, "and go over it."

"It's November, Jesse," Simpson said. "Nobody uses it anyway."

"This guy did," Jesse said.

3

When he left the beach, Jesse called Marcy Campbell on his cell phone.

"I'm up early fighting crime," Jesse said. "Got time for breakfast?"

"It's seven-thirty in the morning," Marcy said. "What if I'd been asleep?"

"You'd be dreaming of me. When's your first appointment."

"I'm showing a house on Paradise Neck at eleven," Marcy said.

"I'll come by for you."

"I'm just out of the shower," Marcy said. "I'm not even dressed."

"Good," Jesse said. "I'll hurry."

Sitting across from Jesse in the Indigo Apple Café at 8:15, Marcy was completely put together. Her platinum hair was perfectly in place. Her makeup was flawless.

"You got ready pretty fast," Jesse said.

"Crime busters float my boat," Marcy said. "What are you doing so early."

"Found a body on the beach," Jesse said.

"Town beach?"

"Yes. He'd been shot twice."

"My God," Marcy said. "Who was it."

"Don't know yet," Jesse said. "ME is looking at him now."

"Do you get help on major crimes like that?"

"If we need it," Jesse said.

"Oh dear," Marcy said. "I've stepped on a prickle."

"We're a pretty good little operation here," Jesse said. "Admittedly we don't have all the resources of a big department. State cops help us out on that."

"And you don't like it when that happens."

"I like to run my own show," Jesse said. "When I can."

The Indigo Apple had a lot of etched glass and blue curtains. For breakfast it specialized in omelets with regional names. Italian omelets with tomato sauce, Mexican omelets with cheese and peppers, Swedish omelets with sour cream and mushrooms. Jesse chose a Mexican omelet. Marcy ordered wheat toast.

"Speaking of which, how is the drinking?"

"Good," Jesse said.

He didn't like to talk about his drinking, even to Marcy.

"And the love life?" Marcy said.

"Besides you?"

"Besides me."

"Various," Jesse said.

"Well, doesn't that make me feel special," Marcy said.

"Oh God, don't you get the vapors on me," Jesse said.

"No." Marcy smiled. "I won't. We're not lovers. We're pals who fuck."

"What are pals for," Jesse said.

"It's why we get along."

"Because we don't love each other?"

"It helps," Marcy said. "How's the ex-wife?"

"Jenn," Jesse said.

"Jenn."

Jesse leaned back a little and looked past Marcy through the etched glass front window of the café at people going by on the street, starting the day.

"Jenn," he said again. "Well . . . she doesn't seem to be in love with that anchorman anymore."

"Was she ever?"

"Probably not."

Marcy ate some toast and drank some coffee.

"She's going out with some guy from Harvard," Jesse said.

"A professor?"

The waitress stopped by the table and refilled their coffee cups.

"No, some sort of dean, I think."

"Climbing the intellectual ladder," Marcy said.

Jesse shrugged.

"You've been divorced like five years," Marcy said.

"Four years and eleven days."

Marcy stirred her coffee. "I'm older than you are," Marcy said.

"Which gives you the right to offer me advice," Jesse said.

"Yes. It's a rule."

"And you advise me," Jesse said, "to forget about Jenn."

"I do," Marcy said.

Jesse cut off a corner of his omelet and ate it and drank some coffee and patted his lips with his napkin.

"Is there anyone advising you otherwise?" Marcy said.

"No."

"If you resolved this thing with Jenn," Marcy said, "maybe you could put the drinking issue away too, and just be a really good police chief."

"I've never been drunk on the job," Jesse said.

"You've never been drunk on the job here," Marcy said.

"Good point," Jesse said softly.

"It got you fired in LA," Marcy said. "After you broke up with Jenn in LA. And you came here to start over."

Jesse nodded

Marcy said, "So?"

"So?"

"So Jenn followed you here and you still struggle with booze," Marcy said. "Maybe there's a connection."

Jesse ate some more of his omelet.

"You think anyone in Mexico ever ate an omelet like this?" he said.

"Are you suggesting I shut up?"

Jesse smiled at her and drank some coffee from the big white porcelain mug like the ones they had used in diners when he was a kid, in Tucson.

Jesse shook his head.

"No," he said. "Your advice is good. It's just not good for me."

"Because?"

"I will not give up on Jenn until she gives up on me," Jesse said.

"Isn't that giving her a license to do whatever she wants to and hang on to you?"

"Yes," Jesse said. "It is."

Marcy stared at him.

"How does it make you feel that she's sleeping with other men?" Marcy said.

"We're divorced," Jesse said. "She's got every right."

"Un-huh," Marcy said. "But how does it make you *feel?*"

"It makes me want to puke," Jesse said. "It makes me want to kill any man she's with."

"But you don't."

"Nope."

"Because it's against the law?"

"Because it won't take me where I want to go," Jesse said.

"I don't mean this in any negative way," Marcy said. "You are maybe the simplest person I ever met."

"I know what I want," Jesse said.

"And you keep your eye on the prize," Marcy said.

"I do," Jesse said.

4

Bob Valenti came into Jesse's office and sat down. He was overweight with a thick black beard, wearing a blue windbreaker across the back of which was written *Paradise Animal Control*.

"How you doing, Skipper?" he said.

Valenti was a part-time dog officer and he thought he was a cop. Jesse found him annoying, but he was a pretty good dog officer. In the fifteen years he'd been a cop, dating back to Los Angeles, South Central, Jesse had never heard a commander called Skipper.

"We're pretty informal here, Bob," Jesse said. "You can call me Jesse."

"Sure, Jess, just being respectful."

"And I appreciate it, Bob," Jesse said. "What's up?"

"Picked up a dog this morning," Valenti said, "a vizsla—medium-sized Hungarian pointer, reddish gold in color . . ."

"I know what a vizsla is," Jesse said.

"Anyway, neighbors said he's been hanging around outside a house in the neighborhood for a couple days."

Jesse nodded. Jesse noticed that the sun coming in through the window behind him glinted on some gray hairs in Valenti's beard.

"Not like it used to be," Valenti said. "Dogs running loose they could be lost for days before anybody notices. Now, with the leash laws, people notice any dog that's loose."

Jesse said, "Um-hmm."

"So I go down," Valenti said, "and he's there, hanging around this house on Pleasant Street that's been condo-ed. And he's got that wild look they get. Restless, big eyes, you can tell they're lost."

Jesse nodded.

"So I approach him, easy like, but he's skittish as a bastard," Valenti said. "I had a hell of a time corralling him."

"But you did it," Jesse said, his face blank.

"Oh sure," Valenti said. "I been doing this job a long time."

"Dog got any tags?"

"Yeah. That's the funny thing. He lived there."

"Where?"

"The house he was hanging around. Belongs to somebody named Kenneth Eisley at that address. So I ring the bell, and there's no answer. And I notice that the *Globe* from yesterday and today is there on the porch, like, you know, nobody's home."

"How's the dog?" Jesse said.

"He's kind of scared, you know, ears down, tail down. But he seems healthy enough. I fed him, gave him some water."

"He look well cared for?"

"Oh, yeah. Nice collar, clean. Toenails clipped recently. Teeth are in good shape."

"You pay attention," Jesse said.

"I got an eye for detail," Valenti said. "Part of the job."

"Where's the dog now?"

"I got some kennel facilities in my backyard," Valenti said. "I'll keep him there until we find the owner."

"You got an address for Kenneth Eisley?"

"Yeah, sure. Forty-one Pleasant Street. Big gray house with white trim got three different condo entrances."

"The address will help me find it," Jesse said.

"You got it, Skip," Valenti said.

5

They sat in the study looking at digital pictures on the computer screen.

"Look at them," she said. "Aren't they sweet."

"Your photography is improving," he said.

"Maybe it would be more fun to do a woman this time," she said.

"Variety is the spice of life," he said.

"Any of these look interesting?" she said.

He smiled at her.

"They all look interesting," he said.

"But we need to find the right one," she said.

"Wouldn't want to rush it."

"She may not even be in this batch."

"Then we'll do some more research and come back with a new batch."

"That will be fun," she said.

"It's all fun," he said.

"It is," she said, "isn't it. The research, the selection, the planning, the stalking . . ."

"Every good thing benefits from foreplay," he said.

"The longer you wait for the orgasm, the better it is."

They looked at the slide show some more, the new picture clicking onto the screen every five seconds.

"Stop it there," she said.

"Her?"

"You think?" she said.

"Un-uh."

"Too old?"

"I think we should get someone young and pretty this time."

"That feels right to me," she said.

"Feels good, doesn't it," he said.

"Yes."

He clicked on the slide show again and they sat holding hands watching the images of young men, old men, young women, old women, men and women of indeterminate age. All of them white, except for one Asian man in a blue suit.

"There," he said and froze the image.

"Her?" she said.

"She's the one," he said.

"You think she's good-looking?"

"I think she's great-looking."

"She looks kind of horsy to me."

"She's the one," he said.

He was very firm about it, and she heard the firmness in his voice. He said it again.

"She's the one."

"Okay," his wife said. "You want her, you got her. She does look like she'd be kind of fun."

"That's her house she's coming out of," he said. "Rose Avenue if I remember right."

His wife looked at the list of locations.

"Rose Avenue," she said.

"Memory like a steel trap," he said.

"So tomorrow we put her under surveillance?"

"We watch her every minute of her day," he said. "See who she lives with, when she's alone, where she goes, when. Does she drive? Ride a bike? Jog? Fool around?"

"The more we know," she said, "the more certain it'll be when we do it."

"And the better it will feel."

He smiled. "During or after?" he said.

"Both."

6

Carrying a tan briefcase, Jesse stood on the big wrap-around porch at 41 Pleasant Street. There were two doors that opened onto the porch in front, and one that provided entry from the driveway side. Jesse rang the bell at 41A, where the name under the bell button said *Kenneth Eisley*. He waited. Nothing. The name at 41B was Angie Aarons. He rang the bell, and heard footsteps almost at once. A woman opened the door. She was wearing a black leotard top and baggy gray sweatpants. Her blond hair was pinned up. Her feet were bare. There was a faint sheen of sweat on her face.

"Hello," she said.

"Ms. Aarons?"

"Yes."

Jesse was wearing jeans and his softball jacket. He held up his badge.

"Jesse Stone," he said.

"Could I see that badge again?" she said.

"Sure."

She studied it for a moment.

"You're the chief," she said.

"I am."

"How come you're not wearing a chief suit," she said.

"Casual Tuesday," Jesse said.

"Aren't you awful young to be chief."

"How old is a chief supposed to be?"

"Older than me," she said and smiled.

"I'll do my best," Jesse said. "Are you friendly with Kenneth Eisley, next door?"

"Kenny? Sure, I mean casually. We'd have a drink now and then, sign for each other's packages, stuff like that."

"Have you seen him recently?"

"Not for a couple of days." She paused. "Omigod, where are my manners," she said. "Come in, want some coffee? It's all made."

"Coffee would be good," Jesse said. "Cream and sugar."

She stepped back from the door and he went in. The walls were white. The trim was white. The furniture was bleached oak. The living room was to the right, through an archway. There was a big-screen television to the left of the fireplace, and an exercise mat spread on the rug. She brought him coffee in a large colorful mug.

"I'm sorry," she said. "The good china is in the dishwasher."

"I'm a cop," Jesse said. "All I know how to drink from is Styrofoam."

On the floor near the exercise mat were several pieces of rubber tubing, and a round metal band with rubber grips. She sat on a big white hassock.

"Why are you asking about Kenny," she said.

"He has a dog?"

"Goldie," she said. "He's a vizsla. You know what they are?"

Jesse nodded.

"Goldie's been hanging around outside looking lost for a couple of days," Jesse said. "The dog officer picked him up, but he can't locate Kenny."

"Last I saw they were going over to the beach together to run."

"When was that?" Jesse said.

"Couple nights ago."

Jesse took an eight-by-ten photograph from the briefcase.

"I'm going to show you a picture. It's not gruesome, but it's a picture of a dead person."

"Is it Kenny?"

"That's what you're going to tell me," Jesse said. "You ready?"

She nodded. He held the picture out and she looked at it without taking it, then looked away quickly and sat back.

"Oh," she said. "Oh."

Jesse waited.

After a moment, she nodded.

"Yes," she said. "It's Kenny."

Jesse put the photograph away.

"What happened?" she said.

"Somebody shot him," Jesse said. "On Paradise Beach two nights ago."

"My God, why?"

"Don't know."

"Do you know who?" she said.

Jesse shook his head.

"Goldie," Angie Aarons said. "He must have been running with Kenny on the beach and was there . . ."

"Probably," Jesse said.

"And then he didn't know what to do and he came home . . . poor thing."

"Yes," Jesse said. "Do you have any idea who might want to shoot Kenny?"

"Jesus, no," Angie said.

"What does he do?"

"Ah, he's, ah, he's a, you know, stock guy, some big brokerage in town."

"Family?"

"I don't know. I didn't know him real well. I never saw any family around."

23

"Do you know how long he's lived here?" Jesse said.

"No. He was here when I moved in three years ago."

"From where?"

"From where did I move?"

"Yes."

She smiled.

"Am I a suspect?"

"No," Jesse said. "The question was unofficial."

"Really?" she said. "I came from LA."

"Me too," Jesse said.

7

Jesse was eating a pastrami sandwich on light rye at his desk, when Molly brought the girl and her mother into his office just after noontime on Thursday.

"I think you need to talk with these ladies," Molly said.

Jesse took a swallow of Dr. Brown's Cream Soda. He nodded.

"Excuse my lunch," he said.

"I don't care about your damned lunch," the mother said. "My daughter's been raped."

"Moth-er!"

"You might want to stick around, Molly," Jesse said.

Molly nodded and closed the door and leaned on the wall beside it.

"Tell me about the rape," Jesse said.

"I didn't get raped," the girl said.

"Shut up," the mother said.

Jesse took a bite of his sandwich and chewed quietly.

"She came home from school early and tried to slip into the house. Her dress was torn, her hair was a mess, her lip was swollen. You can still see it. She was crying and she wouldn't tell me why."

Jesse nodded. He drank a little more cream soda.

"I insisted on examining her," the mother said. "She had no underwear, her thighs are bruised. I said I would take her to the doctor if she didn't tell me, so she confessed."

"That she'd been raped?" Jesse said.

He was looking at the daughter. The daughter looked frantic to him.

"Yes."

"Anyone do a rape kit?"

"Excuse me?"

"Did you take her to the doctor," Jesse said.

"And have it all over town, God no. I had her clean herself up and brought her straight to you."

"Clean herself up?"

"Of course. Who knows what germs were involved. And I'm not bringing her in here looking like a refugee."

"Bath?" Jesse said to the daughter. "Shower?"

The daughter wouldn't speak.

"I put her in a hot bath," her mother said, "scrubbed her myself like she was two years old."

Peripherally, Jesse saw Molly raise her eyebrows.

"What are your names," Jesse said.

The mother looked startled, as if Jesse had been impolite.

"I'm Mrs. Chuck Pennington. This is Candace."

Jesse said, "So who raped you, Candy?"

"Candace," her mother said.

Jesse nodded.

"Candace," he said.

Candace shook her head.

"You tell him, young lady. I will not permit anyone to rape my daughter and think they can get away with it."

"I won't tell," Candace said. "You can't make me."

"No," Jesse said, "I can't. But it's hard to protect you if I don't know who they are."

"You can't protect me," Candace said.

"He threaten you?"

"They all did."

"All," her mother said, "dear God in Heaven. You tell the chief right now what happened."

Candace shook her head. Her face was red. She was teary.

"If I don't know who they are," Jesse said, "I can't stop them. They might do it again. To another girl. To you."

Candace shook her head.

"Don't you even want revenge," Molly said. "If it happened to me I'd want revenge. I'd want them caught."

Candace didn't speak. Her mother slapped her on the back of her head.

"No hitting," Jesse said. "Molly, why don't you take Candace out to the conference room."

Molly nodded. Left the wall and put her hand gently under Candace's left arm and helped her out of the chair and through Jesse's office door. Jesse got up and went around to the door and closed it and came back to his desk.

"She's been traumatized by the rapists," Jesse said. "She should not be traumatized by her mother."

"Don't you dare tell me how to raise my daughter."

"I don't know a hell of a lot about daughters," Jesse said. "But I know something about rapes. She needs to see a doctor. If nothing else he might be able to give her some sedation. Who's her gynecologist? I can call him for you."

"Is there some kind of medical thing they can find out who did it."

"The hot bath tends to wash away evidence," Jesse said.

"Well then, I won't take her. The doctor may not tell, but someone will. The nurse, the receptionist. The doctor's husband. I am not going to have her the subject of a lot of filthy talk all over town."

Jesse finished his pastrami sandwich and drank the last of his cream soda and wiped his mouth with a paper napkin. He put the napkin and the empty can and the sandwich wrapper in the wastebasket. He rocked his chair back and rested one foot on the open bottom file drawer in his desk, and tapped his fingers gently on the flat of his stomach, and looked thoughtfully at Mrs. Pennington.

"Why don't I talk to her alone," he said.

"You think she'll tell you things she won't tell her own mother?"

"Sometimes people do," Jesse said.

Mrs. Pennington frowned. She put her palms together and tapped her upper lip with the tips of her fingers. She's pretty good-looking, Jesse thought. A little too blond, a little too tan, a little too carefully done, maybe, teeth a little too white. Face is kind of mean, but a good body.

"This entire incident must remain confidential," Mrs. Pennington said.

Jesse nodded.

"Can you promise me that?"

Jesse shook his head.

"You can't?"

"Of course not. We don't plan to blab about it. But, if there are arrests, indictments, trials, someone will hear about it."

"Oh God," she said. "I cannot bear, *cannot bear,* the scandal."

"Being raped is not scandalous behavior," Jesse said.

"You don't understand."

Jesse didn't say anything.

"I can't discuss this any further. I'm taking my daughter home."

"Sooner or later you'll have to deal with this," Jesse said. "Or she will."

"I want my daughter," she said.

Jesse stood and went to his office door.

He yelled, "Molly," and when she appeared he said, "Bring the girl in."

When she saw her daughter, Mrs. Pennington stood.

"We'll go home now," she said.

Candace's eyes were red and swollen. A bruise had begun to darken on her cheekbone. She seemed disconnected. Jesse looked at Molly. Molly shook her head.

"Candace," Jesse said.

The girl looked at him vaguely. Her pupils were large. She had no focus.

"Is there anything you want to say to me?" Jesse said.

She looked at her mother.

"We are through here, Candace," Mrs. Pennington said.

The girl looked back at Jesse. Their eyes met and held for a moment. Jesse thought he saw for just a moment a stir of personhood in there. Jesse nodded slightly. The girl didn't say anything. Then her mother took her arm and they walked out of the station.

8

"I'm here to cook you supper," Jenn said when she arrived at Jesse's condo with a large shopping bag.

"Cook?" Jesse said.

"I can cook," Jenn said.

"I didn't know that," Jesse said.

"I've been taking a course," Jenn said and set the shopping bag down on the counter in Jesse's kitchen. "Perhaps you could make us a cocktail?"

"I could," Jesse said.

Jenn took a small green apron out of the shopping bag and tied it on.

"Serious," Jesse said.

"Dress for success," Jenn said and smiled at him.

Jesse made them martinis. Jenn put some grilled shrimp and mango chutney on a glass plate. They took the drinks and the hors d'oeuvres to the living room and sat on Jesse's sofa and looked out the slider over Jesse's balcony to the harbor beyond.

"It's pretty here, Jesse."

"Yes."

"But it's so . . . stark."

"Stark?"

"You know, the walls are white. The tabletops are bare. There's no pictures."

"There's Ozzie," Jesse said.

Jenn looked at the big framed color photograph of Ozzie Smith, in midair, stretched parallel to the ground, catching a baseball.

"You've had that since I've known you."

"Best shortstop I ever saw," Jesse said.

"You might have been that good, if you hadn't gotten hurt."

Jesse smiled and shook his head.

"I might have made the show," Jesse said. "But I wouldn't have been Ozzie."

"Anyway," Jenn said. "One picture of a baseball player is not interior decor."

"Picture of you in my bedroom," Jesse said. "On the table."

"What do you do with it if you have a sleepover?"

"It stays," Jesse said. "Sleepovers have to know about you."

"Is that in your best interest?" Jenn said. "Wouldn't it discourage sleeping over."

"Maybe," Jesse said.

"But not entirely," Jenn said.

"No," Jesse said. "Not entirely."

They were silent, thinking about it. Jesse got up and made another shaker of martinis.

"What is it they have to know about me?" Jenn said when he brought the shaker back.

"That I love you, and, probably, am not going to love them."

"Good," Jenn said.

"Good for who?" Jesse said.

"For me at least," Jenn said. "I want you in my life."

"Are you sure divorcing me is the best way to show that?"

"I can't imagine a life without you in it."

"Old habits die hard," Jesse said.

"It's more than a habit, Jesse. There's some sort of connection between us that won't break."

"Maybe its because I don't let it break," Jesse said.

"You don't," Jenn said. "But then here I am."

"Here you are."

"I could have been a weather girl in Los Angeles, or Pittsburgh or San Antonio."

"But here you are," Jesse said.

"You're not the only one hanging on," Jenn said.

"What the hell is wrong with us?" Jesse said.

Jenn put her glass out. Jesse freshened her drink.

"Probably a lot more than we know," Jenn said. "But one thing I do know: we take it seriously."

"What?"

"Love, marriage, relationship, each other."

"Which is why we got divorced and started fucking other people," Jesse said. "Or vice versa."

"I deserve the vice versa," Jenn said. "But I don't keep deserving it every time we talk."

"I know," Jesse said. "I'm sorry. But if we take it so seriously, why the hell are we in this mess."

"Because we wouldn't let it slide," Jenn said. "Because you wouldn't accept adultery. Because I wouldn't accept suffocation."

"I loved you very intensely," Jesse said.

There was half a drink left in the shaker. Jesse added it to his glass.

"You loved your fantasy of me very intensely," Jenn said, "and kept trying to squeeze the real me into that fantasy."

Jesse stared at the crystalline liquid in his glass. Jenn was still. Below them the harbor master's launch pulled away from the town pier and began to weave through the stand of masts going somewhere, *and knowing where.*

"That you talking or the shrink?" Jesse said.

"It's a conclusion we reached together," Jenn said.

Jesse hated all the circumlocutions of therapy. He sipped the lucid martini.

"Why do you think I'm so wonderful?" Jenn said.

"Because I love you."

Jenn was quiet. She smiled slightly as if she knew something Jesse didn't know. It annoyed him.

"What the fuck is wrong with that?" he said.

"Think about it," Jenn said.

"Think about shit," Jesse said. "Just because you're getting shrunk doesn't mean you have to shrink me."

"You think I'm wonderful because you love me?"

"Yes."

They were both quiet. Jesse stared at her defiantly. Jenn looking faintly quizzical.

After a time, Jenn said, "Not the other way around?"

Jesse nodded slowly as if to himself, then got up and mixed a new martini.

9

Jesse's hangover was relentless on Monday morning. He sat behind his desk sipping bottled water and trying to concentrate on Peter Perkins.

"We spent two days going over that guy's apartment," Perkins said. "We didn't even find anything embarrassing."

"And him a stockbroker," Jesse said. "So what do you know?"

Perkins looked down at his notebook.

"Kenneth Eisley, age thirty-seven, divorced, no children. Works for Hollingsworth and Whitney in Boston. Parents live in Amherst. They've been notified."

"You do that?"

"Molly," Peter Perkins said.

"God bless her," Jesse said.

"Coroner's through with him," Perkins said. "Parents are coming tomorrow to claim the body. You want to talk to them?"

"You do it," Jesse said.

"You pulling rank on me?" Perkins said.

"You bet," Jesse said. "How about the ex-wife?"

"She lives in Paradise," Perkins said. "On Plum Tree Road. Probably kept the house when they split."

"Seen her yet?"

"No. Hasn't returned our calls."

"I'll go over," Jesse said.

"Swell," Perkins said. "I get to question the grieving parents, you talk to the ex-wife, who is probably delighted."

"Not if she was getting alimony," Jesse said.

"That's cynical," Peter Perkins said.

"It is," Jesse said. "What's the ME say?"

"Nothing special. Shot twice in the chest at close range. Two different guns."

"Two guns?"

"Yep. Both twenty-twos."

"Which one killed him?"

"Both."

"Equally?"

"Either shot would have done it. They both got him in

the heart. You want all the details about what got penetrated and stuff?"

"I'll read the report. We figure two shooters?"

"Can't see why one guy would shoot someone with two guns," Perkins said.

"Any way to tell which one shot first?"

"Not really. Far as the ME could tell they entered the victim more or less the same time."

"Both at close range," Jesse said.

"Both at close range."

"Both in the heart," Jesse said.

Perkins nodded. "Gotta be two people," he said.

"Or one person who wants us to think he's two people," Jesse said.

Perkins shrugged.

"Pretty elaborate," Perkins said. "And it gives us twice as many murder weapons."

Jesse drank more spring water. He didn't say anything.

"We got his phone records," Perkins said. "Anthony and Suit are chasing that down."

"Debt?" Jesse said.

"Not so far. Got ten grand in his checking account. Got a mutual fund worth couple hundred thousand. I'm telling you, we've got nada."

"Somebody killed him and they had a reason," Jesse said. "Talk to people where he worked?"

"No. I was going to ask you. Should I call, or go in to Boston."

"Go in," Jesse said. "It's harder to brush you off."

"You did a lot of this in LA," Perkins said. "You got any ideas."

"When in doubt," Jesse said, "cherchez la ex-wife."

"Wow," Perkins said, "it's great working with a pro."

10

She was taking the photographs of Kenneth Eisley down from the big oak-framed corkboard in the office.

"Leave that head shot," he said.

"Memories?" she said.

"Trophy," he said.

She smiled, and handed him the pile of discarded pictures.

"Shred these," she said. "While I put up the new pictures."

He began to feed the discarded photographs through the shredder.

"What is our new friend's name?" she said.

"Barbara Carey," he said. "Forty-two years old, married, no children. Her husband's name is Kevin. She's a loan officer at the in-town branch of Pequot. He's a lawyer in Danvers."

"They happy?"

"What's happy?" he said. "They go out every Saturday night, usually with friends. They go to brunch a lot of Sundays. The second picture up, they're coming out of the Four Seasons. They don't fight in public. They both drink, but neither one seems to be a drunk."

"They own a dog?" she said.

"No sign," he said. "I think they're too busy being successful young professionals to get tied down by a dog."

"That's good," she said. "I still feel worried about Kenny's dog."

She glanced at the remaining photograph of Kenneth Eisley.

"Somebody will find the dog and adopt him," he said.

"I hope so," she said. "Dogs are nice."

He fed the last photograph into the shredder.

"Kevin usually leaves the house first in the morning," he said. "She leaves about a half hour later, at eight-thirty."

"That means she's home alone for half an hour every weekday morning."

"Yes, but it's a neighborhood where everyone is home looking out the window," he said.

"So where will we be able to do it?"

"She does the food shopping," he said.

"At the Paradise Mall," she said.

She pinned the last of the pictures onto the corkboard with a small red map tack, then stepped back beside him and the two of them looked at thirty-five photographs of Barbara Carey going about the business of her public life.

"Big parking lot," he said. "At the Paradise Mall."

11

Molly Crane had a pretty good body, Jesse thought, for a cop with three kids. The gun belt always looked too big for her. She adjusted it as she sat in the chair across from Jesse's desk.

"I've been doing a little off-hours snooping," Molly said.

Jesse waited.

"Into the rape thing."

"Candace Pennington," Jesse said.

"Yes."

"How you doing?" Jesse said.

"Well," Molly said, "mostly I'm just watching. I park outside in my own car, no uniform, and watch her come to school, and go home. During lunch hour, I hang out in the cafeteria kitchen and watch. I know the food service lady down there, Anne Minnihan."

"Find out anything?"

"Maybe," Molly said. "There was a moment this morning in the cafeteria. Three boys sort of circled her and they stood and talked for maybe two minutes. They were all big and she was against the wall, and you could barely see her. One of them showed her something. The boys laughed. Then they moved away."

"How did Candace react."

"Scared."

"You're sure?"

"Yes. She was terrified, and . . . something else."

"Something else?"

"Yes. I can't quite say what. It was like whatever they'd shown her was . . . horrifying."

"Know the boys?" Jesse said.

"Not by name, yet," Molly said. "But I'd recognize all of them."

"Okay," Jesse said. "We don't want to cause this kid any more pain than she's already in. You need to ID these three boys without them knowing it."

"They were big, one of them was wearing a varsity jacket. I'll check the sports team photos in the lobby," Molly said.

"Out of uniform," Jesse said. "Just a suburban mom waiting to see the guidance counselor."

"Hey," Molly said. "I'm not old enough to have kids in high school."

"Vanity, vanity," Jesse said.

"Cops can be vain," Molly said.

"Sure," Jesse said.

"You're thinking *especially if they're female,* aren't you?"

Jesse leaned back in his chair and put his hands up.

He said, "I don't have a sexist bone in my body, cutie pie."

"Anyway," Molly said, "I've lived in this town my whole life. I'll get them ID'd."

"Okay, as long as you keep the kid in mind."

"Candace?"

"Yes."

"Hard to investigate a crime without anyone knowing it," Molly said. "For crissake, we can't even talk to the victim."

Jesse smiled. "Hard, we do at once," he said. "Impossible takes a little longer."

"Oh God," Molly said, "spare me."

Jesse grinned. "Just be careful of Candace," he said.

"You're very soft-hearted, Jesse."

"Sometimes," he said.

12

Kenneth Eisley's former wife had resurrected her maiden name, which was Erickson. She worked as a corporate trainer at a company called Prometheus Plus, which was located in an office park in Woburn, and Jesse talked to her there, sitting in a chair made of silver tubing across from her desk. The desk too was made of silver tubing, with a glass top.

"Do you have any idea why someone might kill your former husband?" Jesse said.

Christine Erickson laughed briefly and without amusement.

"Other than for being a jerk?" she said.

"Was he enough of a jerk to get himself shot?"

"Not that kind of jerk," she said. "He was a harmless jerk."

"Such as?" Jesse said.

"He thought it was important, I mean he actually thought it was seriously important, who won the Super Bowl."

"Everybody knows it's the World Series that matters," Jesse said.

Christine looked blankly at Jesse for a moment. Jesse smiled. Her demeanor was calm enough, Jesse noticed, but her movements seemed tight and angular.

"Oh," she said. "You're kidding."

"More or less," Jesse said. "What else was annoying about him?"

Christine was wearing a dark maroon pantsuit with a white blouse and short cordovan boots with pointy toes and heels a little too high to be sensible. She was slim and good-looking, with auburn hair and oval wire-rimmed glasses. Behind the glasses, her eyes were greenish.

"He believed the ads on television," she said without hesitation.

She's talked about his faults before, Jesse thought.

"He thinks what matters is looking good, knowing the right people, driving the right car, owning the right dog. . . . Oh God, what about Goldie?"

"He's healthy," Jesse said. "Dog officer has him."

"What's going to happen to him?"

"I was hoping you'd take him," Jesse said.

"Me. God no. I can't. I work twelve hours a day."

Jesse nodded.

"Can you find him a home?" Christine said.

Jesse nodded.

"You think I should take him," Christine said, "don't you?"

"I do," Jesse said.

"I can't have him home alone all day, peeing on my rugs."

Jesse nodded.

"Well, I can't," Christine said.

"'Course not," Jesse said.

"Hell, he was never my dog. Kenny just bought him because he thought they'd look good running on the beach together."

"They do that often?"

"Five nights a week," she said. "Kenny was always obsessing about his weight."

"Regular?"

"Kenny? Oh, God, yes, he was a schedule freak. Same time for everything. Always." Suddenly she smiled a thin smile. "I mean everything."

"Good to know," Jesse said. "Do you have any idea who would want him dead?"

"Oh," she said, "God no."

"Does he pay you alimony?"

"No. I got my house in lieu of alimony. Hell, I make more than he does anyway."

"Where were you last Thursday night?" Jesse said.

"Me?"

"Have to ask," Jesse said.

She glanced at her date book, then looked up and met his gaze for a moment. He could see her thinking.

She said, "I was in bed with Neil Ames."

"All night?"

"We were together from five-thirty in the afternoon until nine A.M. the next morning."

"I'll need to verify it," Jesse said. "Where do I find Mr. Ames?"

"Two doors down," she said. "He's the marketing director."

"Does he think the Super Bowl matters?" Jesse said.

"No."

"What does he think matters?"

"Money."

"No fool, he," Jesse said. "Can you tell me anything at all that might shed light on Kenneth Eisley's death?"

"Have you tried at work?" she said. "Maybe he lost somebody's life savings."

"As we speak," Jesse said. "Any other thoughts?"

"No."

Jesse took a card out of his shirt pocket and handed it to Christine.

"Anything occurs," he said, "call me."

"Even if it's not about the case?"

"Sure," Jesse said. "Maybe we can schedule something."

Again the tight smile. Jesse smiled back. Then he went down the hall to talk with the marketing director.

13

Jesse stood in the living room of Ken Eisley's condominium, listening to the silence. Jesse liked to go alone to places where victims lived, and visit for a while. Rarely did the silence whisper to him anything worth hearing, but that didn't mean it wouldn't, and being there helped him think. The condo was a mirror image of the one where Angie Aarons lived. On the living room floor, near the gas fireplace, was a big plaid dog cushion. On the low oak coffee table was a bottle of single malt scotch and two short thick glasses. Above the fireplace was a four-inch-thin wall-mounted television set that Jesse knew cost about $7,000. On an end table was a baseball enclosed in a plastic case.

The ball had been signed almost illegibly by Willie Mays. To the right of the fireplace was a small maroon and gold replica model of an Indian motorcycle. In the kitchen was a set of stainless steel dog dishes in a black metal rack. There was a king-sized walnut sleigh bed and a large-screen television in the bedroom. On the bedside table were two copies of a magazine about men's health and exercise. In the bathroom was a wooden container of shaving soap, a brush, and a double-edged razor. The razor and the shaving brush each had an ivory handle. A bottle of bay rum stood on the shaving ledge beside them. Everything was obviously new.

The fact that the marketing director had alibied Christine Erickson didn't prove much, Jesse thought. There were probably two people involved in the shooting. And each could be the other's alibi. But why? Jesse could find no reason for either of them to kill Eisley. According to Peter Perkins, Eisley was medium successful. He hadn't made anyone rich, including himself. But he hadn't put anyone in debtors' prison, either. He'd stayed about even with a down market. Maybe he should go in and talk to people himself. Perkins was pretty good, but, like most of the department, he didn't have much experience with homicide investigations.

In the den Jesse found another television and a big sound system. There was a gumball machine, a model of the original Thunderbird, a big illuminated globe, and some sort of glass slab filled with water through which bubbles rose endlessly. *The world according to Sharper Image.*

There were no photographs. There were no books. Jesse

went to Eisley's front porch and checked the mailbox. There was a J. Crew catalogue. Peter Perkins had the checkbook, bills, credit card receipts kind of evidence. He was perfectly competent to evaluate it. What interested Jesse was the emptiness. Except for the dog cushion. There was no hint that anyone lived there and enjoyed it. It was monastically neat. If their timeline was right, Eisley had come home from work, put on his sweats, and gone out for a run with the dog. But there were no clothes draped on a chair or across his bed. Whatever he had worn he had carefully hung up, or put in the laundry bag. His shoes were lined up on the shoe rack in his bedroom closet. The refrigerator was nearly empty. The CD player seemed ornamental. Jesse smiled in the dead silent house.

Not even a picture of Ozzie Smith . . .

Jesse moved slowly from room to room again. He didn't open any drawers or closets. He didn't pick up any artifacts, he simply moved slowly through the house. He saw nothing, smelled nothing, heard nothing, felt nothing that would even hint at why someone had wanted to put two bullets into Kenneth Eisley's chest. The kitchen wall beside the back door had a doggie door cut into it, that led to a fenced run in the backyard.

Maybe I should get a dog.

Jesse had no yard. What would the dog do all day? He sat for a few more moments, then stood and left the empty condo, and locked the door behind him.

14

When Jesse came back to the station Molly was at the front desk, talking on the phone. She made a circle with her thumb and forefinger, holding the other three fingers straight.

"Does that translate to 'I've ID'd the three boys'?" Jesse said.

Molly nodded.

"When you get a break on the desk," Jesse said, "come see me."

Then he went on into the office and closed the door and called Marcy Campbell.

"You free tonight?" he said.

"Yes."

"Can you come over to my place?"

"I'd be foolish not to," Marcy said.

"We can order in," Jesse said.

"Chinese?" Marcy said. "You know how erotic I get when I eat Chinese."

"Or when you don't," Jesse said.

Molly knocked and came into the office and lingered politely by the door until Jesse hung up. Then she sat in the chair across from him, adjusted her handgun so it didn't dig into her lower back, and looked down at her notebook.

"Bo Marino, Kevin Feeney, Troy Drake," she said.

"The three boys you saw hassle Candace."

"Yes."

"Got anything more?"

"Not yet."

"You got a plan?" Jesse said.

"I'm going to haunt them," Molly said.

"You do have to work here sometimes," Jesse said.

"My time," Molly said.

"Company time too," Jesse said, "when we can spare you. It is company business."

"It's woman's business, too," Molly said.

"I understand that."

"I'm not sure you do," Molly said. "I'm not sure any man does."

"I don't like rape much either," Jesse said.

"No. I'm sure you don't. But you haven't lived with it since before you even knew what it was."

"Because it's the worst thing that can happen?"

"No," Molly said. "There are several things worse. It's one reason women submit to it, it's better than the alternative."

"Like death," Jesse said.

"Or torture or both. But rape is the thing your mother was scared of. It's the possibility that you have not only known but felt, since little boys peeked up your dress."

"You knew we did that?" Jesse said.

"Any woman has always known she is the object of sexual interest from almost any man, and that almost any man, if he chooses, can force himself sexually upon her."

"You ever been raped?" Jesse said.

"No. But almost any woman has had more sexual attention from some man than she wanted. We all know about duress."

"Not all of us are, ah, duressful," Jesse said.

"No. But you know what they say—you have to judge what the enemy can do, not what he might do."

"Are we all the enemy?"

"Oh, God, no," Molly said. "I love you, Jesse. . . . And my husband . . ." She paused. "He's my best friend, my lover, my . . ." She shook her head. "But there are things women know that men may never know."

"Which is why you're all over this rape case like ugly on a toad."

"Yes."

"Men may know things women don't," Jesse said.

"I'm sure that is so. But rape is one of the things we know," Molly said.

Jesse nodded. "Control might become sort of an issue for some women," Jesse said.

"If they are with a controlling man," Molly said.

"You do a lot of thinking," Jesse said. "For an Irish Catholic cop."

"An Irish Catholic married female mother of three kids small-town cop," Molly said.

"Exactly," Jesse said.

"So," Molly said, "I'm going to haunt them."

"Just do everything right," Jesse said, "so if they did do it, we don't lose them."

"I know."

"And don't forget that these may be high school kids but they are bigger and stronger than you are."

"It's a thing women never, ever forget," Molly said.

"Duh," Jesse said. "I guess that's pretty much what you've been telling me."

"Pretty much," Molly said, and smiled at him. "Don't get nervous, though. I won't keep telling you."

15

The woman's body lay on its side, at the far end of the parking lot in the Paradise Mall. Her head was jammed against the rear tire of a silver Volvo Cross Country wagon. A shopping cart full of groceries stood nose-in against the black Audi sedan next to the Volvo. Jesse sat on his heels beside Peter Perkins and looked at her.

"Two in the chest," Perkins said. "Look like small-caliber to me."

"Just like Kenneth Eisley," Jesse said.

"At first look," Perkins said.

"Keys were in her hand," Jesse said. "And she dropped them when she was shot."

"She probably popped the rear gate with the remote on her key chain," Perkins said. "Rear gate is unlatched but not open."

Jesse looked at the unemptied shopping cart. Behind them several people, attracted by the blue lights on the patrol cars, stood in silence, held away from the crime scene by Simpson and deAngelo. In the distance a siren sounded.

"That'll be the EMTs," Perkins said.

"She doesn't need them anymore."

"No," Perkins said. "But they can haul her away."

Jesse nodded.

"So," he said. "She food shops in the market. And checks out and wheels her cart out here. . . . This her car?"

"I assume so."

"Try her keys," Jesse said.

Wearing gloves, Perkins picked up the key chain and pointed the remote at the Volvo and clicked the power lock. The lights flashed and the door locks clicked. He unlocked the doors the same way, then dropped the keys into an evidence bag and made a notation on the label.

"Okay, so she comes out here to her car. . . ." He looked around the parking lot. "Which is way out here because the lot is full."

"Friday night," Perkins said.

"It's always like this on a Friday night?"

"Yeah. Worse before a holiday."

"She pops her rear door," Jesse said, "to put her stuff away, and gets two in the chest. She maybe lived five more seconds and turned half away before she died, and fell, and her head jammed up that way against the rear tire."

Perkins nodded.

"That's how I'd read it," he said.

The mercury floods in the parking lot gave everything a faint bluish tinge. In other parts of the lot cars were looking for spots and waiting for people to load their groceries and pull out so that they could pull in. If they saw the blue lights they didn't react, and having places to go, went.

The Paradise emergency response wagon rolled in to a stop and Duke Vincent got out. He knelt beside the woman and felt for a pulse. He knew, as they all knew, that he wouldn't find one. But it was routine. It would be embarrassing to take a living body to the morgue.

"Can we move her yet?" he said to Jesse.

Jesse looked at Perkins. "You all set?" he said.

"Yeah, I've chalked the outline."

"Okay, Dukie," Jesse said.

"She got a name?" Duke said as they loaded her into the back of the wagon.

"Driver's license says Barbara Carey."

Vincent nodded. "You noticed she got shot just like the guy on the beach," he said.

"I noticed," Jesse said.

"Just thought I'd mention it," Duke said, and got in the wagon and drove away.

The people gathered to watch began to drift away. Suitcase Simpson came over to stand with Jesse and Peter Perkins.

"Whaddya think," he said.

He spoke to both of them, but he looked at Jesse.

"Well, there was money still in her purse," Perkins said. "She was still wearing her rings and necklace."

"Unless it was a random shooting," Jesse said, "the killer, or killers, had to follow her here. Even if they knew she was coming here to shop, they'd have no way to know where she'd park."

"Which means they drove," Simpson said.

Jesse nodded.

"And if they drove, they'd park near where she parked and sit in the car and wait for her to come out," Jesse said. "Peter, you and Suit and Anthony get the license numbers of any cars that could see her car from where they were parked."

"You think the killer could still be here?" Simpson said.

"Don't know," Jesse said. "Let's see."

He jabbed his forefinger toward the parked cars.

"You bet," Perkins said.

Jesse went to his car and called Molly on the radio.

"Got a woman shot to death at the mall," he said. "Driver's license says she's Barbara Carey, Sixteen Rose Ave. See if she's got a next of kin."

"If there is, do I notify?" Molly said.

"I'll do that," Jesse said.

"No," Molly said. "I can do it."

"Okay," Jesse said. "Let me know."

Among the few people still watching, a husband and wife held hands and whispered together.

"Who's that talking on the radio?" she said.

"Chief of police, I think."

"He's cute," she said.

"I didn't notice," he said.

"What are the other cops doing," she said.

"Taking down license plates."

"My God," she said. "They'll find our names."

"So," he said. "They'll find a hundred other names too."

"Do you think they'll question us?"

"It's a small-town force," he said. "I doubt they've got the manpower."

"Be kind of exciting if they did," she said.

"Yes."

"What would we say."

"We'd say we came here to pick up some groceries," he said. "Which we did."

"I thought I might have an orgasm right there," she said, "standing beside her putting grapes in a bag."

He smiled and squeezed her hand.

"Up close and personal," he said softly.

16

"For Christ's sake," Marcy said. "You can't have someone to dinner and just plonk three cartons of Chinese food
on the table."

"Of course you can't," Jesse said. "I just wanted to see if
you knew that."

"Yeah, right," Marcy said.

She was looking through his kitchen cabinets.

"You can make us a cocktail," she said. "While I set the
table."

Without asking, Jesse made each of them a tall scotch
and soda.

Holding two wineglasses, Marcy said, "What wine goes with Chinese food?"

"Probably a muscular cabernet," Jesse said.

"Do you have any?"

"No."

"What have you got?"

"Black Label scotch, Absolut vodka, Budweiser beer."

Marcy nodded and put the wineglasses away. She put the cartons of food in a low oven and brought her drink over to the couch.

"How's it going with Jenn?" she said.

Jesse shrugged.

"That well?" Marcy said.

"She came over the other night and cooked me dinner," Jesse said.

"Good dinner?"

"Fancy," Jesse said. "She's taking cooking classes."

"Was the evening all right?"

"Sure," Jesse said.

Marcy was quiet, holding her glass in both hands, sipping.

"This works out very well for her," Marcy said finally.

"What?"

"This arrangement. She has you when she wants you. If she gets in trouble you're there. If she needs sympathy or support or understanding you're there. If she wants to see somebody else, she's free to."

"That's probably true," Jesse said.

"What do you get?" Marcy said.

Jesse went to the kitchen counter and made himself another drink. He brought it back and stood and looked out
his picture window at the harbor.

"I'm in this for the long haul, Marce."

"Which means?"

"Which means, I love her, and I'll stick until she proves
to me that there's no way to fix things."

"And she hasn't?"

"No."

"Does she say she loves you?"

"Yes."

"I don't want to make you mad, but have you thought
she might just be manipulating you?"

"Yes."

"And?"

"And she's not," Jesse said.

Marcy sipped minimally at her scotch.

"Have you seen that shrink lately?"

"Dix? I see him."

"Do you talk about this?"

"Some."

"Am I getting too nosy?" Marcy said.

"Yes."

Marcy took a big swallow of her drink.

"I heard about another murder in town," she said. "Up at
the mall."

Jesse nodded.

"Any luck with it?"

Jesse shook his head.

"How about the other one, the man on the beach?"

"Nope."

"Well," Marcy said, "it's a long season."

"Yes."

They were quiet for a bit. It was full evening, and past where Jesse stood by the window, across the dark harbor, they could see the lights of Paradise Neck and Stiles Island. There was no traffic in the harbor.

"Talk to me a little about rape," Jesse said.

"Rape?"

"Yes."

"It's never really been necessary in my case."

Jesse smiled.

"Molly's working on a rape case. She says it's every woman's fear."

"Well . . ." Marcy paused. Her drink was empty. She held it out and Jesse went to mix her another, and made himself one too.

"I would guess that most women are not unaware of the possibility."

Jesse nodded.

"What's the worst thing about it?" Jesse said. "When you think about it."

"It's not that I wake up every day worrying about rapists."

"I know," Jesse said. "But if you think about it, what would be the worst part."

Marcy put her feet up on the couch and shifted so she

could look more comfortably across the harbor. She drank some scotch, and swallowed and let her breath out audibly.

"If he's not hurting you physically," Marcy said, "I suppose it's being degraded to a thing."

"Tell me about that," Jesse said.

She narrowed her eyes at him.

"You're not some kind of a pervert, are you?"

"I don't think so," Jesse said. "Tell me about being a thing."

"Well, you know, it's a woman being used against her will for a purpose in which she has no part. Hell, the guy's using her to jerk off."

"Or something," Jesse said.

"Literally or figuratively," Marcy said, "you're a thing."

"It's not about you," Jesse said.

"No," Marcy said. "It is entirely about the rapist and you don't matter."

Jesse nodded slowly. He walked from the window and sat on the couch beside Marcy. They were quiet. Marcy leaned her head against Jesse's shoulder. He patted her thigh.

"This isn't just about the rape," Marcy said after a while. "Is it."

"No."

"It's also about Jenn," Marcy said.

Jesse nodded.

"Sometimes I think everything is," he said.

17

Jesse was in the parking lot of the Northeast Mall, talking to Molly on a cell phone.

"Where is she now," he said.

"Just coming out of Macy's."

"She alone?"

"Yes."

"Anyone around you recognize?"

"No. This is the time."

"Okay, pick her up and bring her."

Molly didn't actually have a hold on Candace when they came out of the vast shopping sprawl, but she walked close and a little behind, herding her with her right shoulder like a sheepdog.

"Hop in," Jesse said, when they reached him.

"What do you want?" Candace said.

"We'll talk about it when you get in," Jesse said.

Molly opened the door, Candace got in, Molly closed the door. Through the open window she looked at Jesse. He shook his head.

"Is that smart?" Molly said.

"Probably not," Jesse said. "I'll take it from here."

Molly shrugged and nodded and walked away. Jesse knew she disapproved. Sexual harassment was an easy charge to make against a male cop alone with a woman. Jesse put the car in gear.

"You want to slump down so nobody sees you," Jesse said, "I won't take it personally."

Candace sat with her back to the car window.

"What do you want?"

"To talk," Jesse said. "The elaborate stuff is to make sure no one sees you talking to me."

"Why do you care?"

"I don't care. But I was under the impression you did."

Jesse pulled out of the parking lot and went north on Route 114.

"Where are you taking me?"

"There's a Dunkin' Donuts up here," Jesse said. "We'll have a cup of coffee."

"I don't want to talk with you."

"I know," Jesse said. "But I think you have to."

They were quiet while Jesse drove through the take-out window and got two coffees and four cinnamon donuts. Jesse carefully opened the little window in the plastic top of both cups and handed one to Candace. He sat the donuts on the console between them, leaning against the shotgun that stood in its lock rack against the dashboard.

"Bo Marino," Jesse said. "Kevin Feeney, Troy Drake."

Candace's shoulders hunched, her head went down. She didn't say anything.

"We both know they raped you," Jesse said.

Candace hunched herself tighter.

"And we both know they threatened you about telling."

"How do you know that?"

"I'm the police chief," Jesse said. "I know everything."

"I don't know what you are talking about," Candace said in a small voice, her eyes riveted on her own lap.

Jesse ate half a donut and drank some coffee.

"If you let them," Jesse said, "they will make your life miserable as long as you live in this town."

Candace shook her head.

"If you tell me about it," Jesse said, "I can give you your life back."

"My mother," Candace said.

"I can help you with your mother," Jesse said.

Candace kept staring at her lap. Jesse finished his first donut and drank some more coffee. They were both silent. Candace's hunched shoulders began to shake. She made no sound, but Jesse knew she was crying. He put a hand on her near shoulder.

"Off the record," Jesse said. "Just between you and me. No testifying. Nobody knows you told me."

Her shoulders continued to shake.

"Let it out," Jesse said. "You're safe here. It'll never leave the car."

"Bo's the football captain," Candace said and began to cry outright.

Jesse took some Kleenex out of the glove compartment and put them on the dashboard in front of her. He patted her shoulder.

"He's so strong," she said.

Jesse stopped patting and simply rested his hand on her shoulder.

"You know behind the football field . . . there's this little like valley . . . where the railroad tracks are? . . . They took me there."

She was talking and crying at the same time. Her nose was running. She wiped it with a Kleenex.

"They force you?"

"They just . . . told me to come with them . . . and, you know . . . they are . . . so . . . so important . . . you know?"

Jesse nodded.

"Sure," he said. "I know."

"And . . . they started . . . they started talking . . . dirty and they grabbed me and took my clothes off. . . ."

She stopped talking for a time and sobbed. Jesse waited, his hand gently on her shoulder. Finally she got enough control to talk.

"And they did it," she said.

"All three?" Jesse said softly.

"They took turns. . . . Two holding me down, one doing it."

Jesse put his head back against the car seat and closed his eyes for a moment and took in a lot of air quietly through his nose and let it out. Candace cried, softly now, her hands folded in her lap, her head down.

"They took pictures," she said.

Jesse nodded slowly, his head still back against the car seat, his eyes still closed.

"And they'll pass the pictures around the school," Jesse said. "If you say anything."

"Yes."

"Have you seen the pictures?"

"I saw one," Candace said.

"Are they in the picture?"

"One of them."

"Which one?"

"I don't know," she said. "I couldn't stand to look."

"Do you have the picture?"

"I burned it."

"Too bad," Jesse said. "Might be evidence."

Candace shook her head.

"I didn't want anybody to see it."

"I understand," Jesse said. "They threaten you any other way?"

"They said they'd do it again. You know. If I told. And Bo said next time they'd hurt me."

"Your parents know what happened to you?" Jesse said.

"My mother knows I was raped, but not by who."

"Your father?"

"My mother says we can't tell him."

Candace wiped her eyes and blew her nose. Jesse was still for a moment, staring straight ahead through the car windshield, drumming his fingers on his thighs.

"Okay," he said after a time. "It's our secret."

She nodded. Jesse took a card out of his shirt pocket and wrote his home phone number on the back.

"You can call me anytime," Jesse said. "About anything. It'll be between you and me until you say otherwise."

She took the card.

"What are you going to do?" she said.

"I'm going to keep you out of it," Jesse said. "But I'm going to find a way, sooner or later, to bust all three of them."

"You won't tell," she said.

"No," Jesse said. "I won't."

"I'm so scared," she said.

"I know," Jesse said. "Just remember you're not alone anymore. We're in this together."

She nodded.

"Do you want me to take you home or back to the mall."

"The mall," she said. "I'm meeting my friend there at three."

Jesse finished his coffee and a second donut as he drove back to the mall. When he parked near the entrance she sat for a moment in the car.

"Do you think they'll do it again?" she said.

"I don't know. Try not to be alone with them. Call me whenever you need me."

She nodded silently.

"Thank you," she said.

Jesse smiled at her.

"You and me, babe," he said.

18

Healy came in without knocking and sat down in Jesse's office.

"You called?" he said.

Jesse nodded. "Thanks for coming by," he said.

"Not a sacrifice," Healy said. "You know I live up this way."

"We had a couple of murders," Jesse said.

"I heard," Healy said.

"Sent the slugs over to state forensics and your people tell me they came from the same guns."

"Guns?"

"Yeah. Both victims shot twice, one each from two guns."

Healy frowned. "Two shooters?" he said.

"Or one shooter who wants us to think it was two."

"Links between the victims?" Healy said.

"We can't find any," Jesse said.

"They both live here?"

"Along with twenty thousand other people."

Healy nodded slowly.

"Well, you know how to do this," Healy said. "I am not going to ask you a lot of dumb questions."

"All we got is four bullets," Jesse said. "Twenty-twos."

"That'll narrow it down for you," Healy said.

"People use a twenty-two because they don't know one gun from another and that's what they could get hold of," Jesse said.

"Or they are good at it," Healy said. "And like the twenty-two because it's not as noisy and makes less of a mess."

"And maybe because they like to show off."

"These people seem like they can shoot?"

"They put both bullets right in the same place," Jesse said. "Both victims. Either shot would have killed them."

"So we gotta look for the guns," Healy said.

"It's a start."

"How many twenty-two-caliber firearms would you guess are out there in this great land?"

"Let's assume a couple things," Jesse said. "Let's assume there's two shooters. It's more likely than one shooter, two guns."

"Yeah," Healy said.

"And let's assume that the shooters are from Paradise."

"Because both vics are from Paradise," Healy said.

"No wonder you made captain," Jesse said.

"So we get a list of everyone in Massachusetts who owns a twenty-two," Healy said.

"Or bought twenty-two ammunition."

"And we cross-reference anyone who lives in Paradise," Healy said.

"And then maybe we've got some suspects," Jesse said.

"If the shooters bought in Massachusetts," Healy said. "And if the gun store did the paperwork, and if we didn't lose it in the computer, and if they live in Paradise."

"Hell, we've got them cornered," Jesse said. "Can your people do the clerical work?"

"Am I the homicide commander?" Healy said.

"Can they do it fast?"

"I *am* the homicide commander. I *am not* God."

"I thought they were the same thing," Jesse said.

"Think how disappointed I am," Healy said. "It'll be a long process."

"How long?"

"Long," Healy said.

They were silent for a moment.

"I got a bad little thought," Jesse said.

"About the two guns?" Healy said. "Each vic shot the same way, in the same spot, either shot kills them?"

Jesse nodded.

"Be good if you could speed the process up," Jesse said.

"Do what I can," Healy said.

They were silent, looking at each other.

"You used to play ball," Healy said after a time.

"Yeah, Albuquerque," Jesse said.

"I was with Binghamton," Healy said. "Eastern League."

"You get a sniff at the show?"

Healy shook his head.

"Nope. I was a pitcher, Phillies organization, pretty good. Then I went in the Army and came home and got married and had kids. . . ."

Jesse nodded.

"And it went away," Healy said. "You?"

"Shortstop, tore up my shoulder, and that was the end of that."

"Were you good?" Healy asked.

"Yes."

"Too bad," Healy said. "You play anywhere now?"

"Paradise twi league," Jesse said. "Softball."

"Better than nothing," Healy said.

"A lot better," Jesse said.

19

Jesse sat with Suitcase Simpson in the front seat of Simpson's pickup parked up the street from Candace Pennington's home on Paradise Neck. The weathered shingle house sat up on a rocky promontory on the outer side of the neck overlooking the open ocean.

"She walks from here down to the corner of Ocean Ave. to catch the school bus," Jesse said. "Which Molly will be driving."

"School bus company in on this?" Simpson said.

"No. They think we're trying to catch a drug pusher."

"I used to ride the bus to school," Simpson said. "Lot of shit got smoked on that bus."

"Focus here, Suit," Jesse said. "You'll follow her when she walks to the bus stop, and follow the bus to school and watch her until she's in the building. You go in the building after her and hang around near where she is, and, at the end of the day, reverse the procedure."

"What did you tell the school?"

"Same thing, undercover drug investigation."

"I played football with Marino's older brother," Simpson said. "Half the school knows me. How undercover can it be."

"Suit," Jesse said. "We're not really looking for druggies. It's a cover. It's good if everyone knows you're a cop, as long as they don't know why you're there."

"Which is?"

"To protect Candace Pennington, and, maybe, while we're at it, get something on the three creeps that raped her."

"But no one knows that," Simpson said.

"They threatened her if she told on them," Jesse said. "And I promised her that I'd keep it secret."

"Do I wear my unie?" Simpson said.

"No, I told the school to pretend you were a new member of the custodial staff."

"Janitor?"

"Yep."

"Do I get one of those work shirts that has my name over the pocket?"

"Yeah. Do you want *Suitcase*? Or *Luther*?"

"I should never have told you my real name," Simpson said.

"I'm your chief," Jesse said. "You tell me everything."

"Yeah, well, my mother comes by and sees me sweeping up, I'm gonna refer her to you."

Jesse smiled.

"Kid's alone," Jesse said. "She's been raped. She's afraid it might happen again. She's sixteen years old and afraid, and they've threatened to show her naked pictures to everyone in the high school. She's afraid they'll hurt her. She's afraid of her mother's disapproval, and I don't know where her father stands."

Simpson nodded.

"So we're gonna see that she ain't alone."

Jesse nodded.

"Suit," he said. "You may make detective someday."

"We don't have any detective ranks," Simpson said.

"Well," Jesse said. "If we did."

"Hell," Simpson said. "I already made janitor."

20

Monday through Friday evenings, when Garfield Kennedy got off the commuter train at the Paradise Center Station, he waited for the train to leave, then walked a hundred yards down the tracks and cut through behind the Congregational Church to Maple Street where he lived. This Thursday night was like all the others, except that it was raining, and, as he walked behind the church, a man and a woman approached through the rain and shot him to death without a word.

When Jesse got there he already knew what he'd find. Squatting on his heels in the rain beside Peter Perkins, he saw the two small bullet holes in the chest, one on each side. The blood had seeped through Kennedy's raincoat and been nearly washed away by the rain, leaving only a light pink stain.

"Same thing," Jesse said.

"Name's Kennedy," Peter Perkins said. "He's a lawyer, works in Boston. He lives over there, on Maple. Figure he got off the train, cut through the church parking lot toward his house . . . and never made it."

"Family?" Jesse said.

"Wife, three daughters."

"They know?"

"They came over to see what was going on," Perkins said.

"Christ," Jesse said.

"It wasn't good," Perkins said.

"I'll talk with them," Jesse said.

The rain was washing over Kennedy's face and soaking his hair.

"And they won't have any idea why someone killed him," Jesse said. "And I'll ask if they know Kenneth Eisley or Barbara Carey, and they won't. And we'll find no connection among the three of them and the bullets will be from the same guns that killed the other two."

"You think it's a serial killer, Jesse?"

"Yeah," Jesse said. "Any fix on when it happened?"

"I talked with the pastor of the church and he says that the church music director came in to practice on the organ at about four," Perkins said. "And didn't see anything. So, sometime between four and when the call came in at seven-fifteen. Between four and seven-fifteen there were three commuter trains, the last one at six twenty-three."

"Who found the body," Jesse said.

"Couple kids skateboarding."

"In the dark?"

"The pastor says the parking lot lights are on a timer and they turned on at seven. They never changed the timer for daylight savings."

"The kids still here?"

"Yeah. They're in the cruiser with Eddie."

"Hang on to them."

Jesse stood up. "Don't move a thing," he said. "Everything just the way it is."

"Sure thing," Perkins said. "I still got to take my pictures."

Jesse walked away from the scene, a hundred yards up the railroad tracks to the Paradise Center Station. It was empty and dark. The last train would have been at 6:23. He turned and looked down the tracks. This time of year it would have been dark by six. But if you were used to it, you probably wouldn't have a problem. He started down the tracks. He wasn't used to it, but the light from the church parking lot was helpful. *Besides, I'm a natural athlete.* There was a pathway through the screen of trees into the back of the church parking lot. *He walked through this way, carrying his briefcase. Lot was still dark. He's walking down here, toward Maple Street, and he sees a couple people walking toward him, and he doesn't pay any attention and then they get close and bang. He falls pretty much straight backward and, unless they weren't shooting as good as usual, was dead before he was through falling.* He stood over the dead man and looked around the parking lot. There was a maroon Chevrolet Cavalier parked close to the church, and a brown Toyota Camry beside it. All the other vehicles were police and fire vehicles, lights on, flashers flashing. *I wonder why cops always do that. I wonder why we don't shut the damn things off when we get there.* He turned slowly and looked around the parking lot. Across from him was the exit onto Sea Street. To the right a path led through another small screen of trees to Maple Street. Jesse walked to the exit and looked at Sea Street. To the left took you out of town, heading for Route 1. To the right was downtown and the waterfront. He walked back and through the path to Maple Street. Front lawns, driveways, garrison colonials. To the right, near the end of the street, one of the houses was more brightly lit than the others, with several cars parked out front. *Kennedy's house?*

"You know which house is Kennedy's?" Jesse said.

"No, I can ask Anthony."

Jesse shook his head.

"Okay," he said to Perkins. "You can close it up."

Perkins nodded.

"I'll talk with those kids," Jesse said.

"First cruiser," Perkins said. "Where the skateboards are."

21

Jesse got into the front seat of the cruiser beside Ed Cox and turned to talk with the boys in back. The boys were about fourteen. They reeked of self-importance. Too bad about the dead guy, but this was the most exciting thing that had ever happened to them.

"My name's Jesse Stone," he said.

"We know who you are."

"Did you tell your story to the officer?" Jesse said.

"Yes."

"And give him your names and addresses?"

"Sure."

"Okay, now I want you to tell me."

"My name's Richard Owens," one of the boys said.

He was short and slim and blond with a slacker haircut and a gold stud in his left earlobe.

"What do they call you?" Jesse said.

"You mean like my nickname?"

Jesse nodded.

"Rick," the boy said. "Or Ricky sometimes."

"You?" Jesse said to the other boy.

He was an olive-skinned kid, with long black hair that had not fared well in the rain.

"Sidney Lessard," the boy said. "They call me Sid."

"Okay, Sid," Jesse said. "Officer Cox will take you someplace else out of the rain—you can use my car, Eddie."

"How come we can't stay together?" Rick said.

"Police procedure," Jesse said.

"What procedure?" Rick said.

"See if you both tell the same story."

"You think we're lying?" Rick said.

"No way to know," Jesse said. "Yet."

"For crissake . . ." Rick said.

"I'll go," Sid said. "We ain't lying. I'll just go with him."

Cox got out of the driver's side and opened the back door. Sid got out and they walked toward Jesse's car. Jesse reached over and shut off the blue light.

"What'd you see, Rick?" Jesse said.

"Me and Sid come over here to skateboard, you know, it's nice pavement, and they got that handicap ramp, and they turn the lights on every night."

"Even in the rain?" Jesse said.

"Yeah, sure, we don't care about rain."

"You got here after the lights were on."

"'Course, you can't board in the dark."

"'Course," Jesse said.

"Anyway, so we're boarding, maybe five minutes, and I come down the ramp and hit a pebble and fall on my ass and the board goes off into the dark. And I go to get it and I see this guy and I yell for Sid and we can tell he's dead, and—"

"How?"

"How what?" Ricky was slightly annoyed at the interruption.

"How'd you know he was dead?"

"I . . . I don't know, you can just tell, you know. Ain't you ever seen dead people?"

"I have," Jesse said.

"And he's got this pink stain like blood on his front," Rick said. "So we run like hell for the church and tell the minister, and he calls the cops, and you guys show up."

"You see anything that might be a clue?" Jesse said.

"I told you all we seen," Rick said.

"Aside from the cop cars," Jesse said. "There's a maroon Chevrolet Cavalier and a brown Toyota Camry in the parking lot now. Did you see any other cars?"

"Just the Saab," Rick said.

"Tell me about the Saab."

"It was a Saab ninety-five sedan, red, with the custom wheel covers."

"Where was it?"

"Parked by the driveway over there, when we come by with our boards."

"Anyone in it?"

"I don't know."

"But you noticed the car and model and wheels," Jesse said.

"Sure, I like cars."

Jesse smiled. "When did it leave?"

"I don't know. After we seen the dead guy and run in the church and told the minister, when we come out again it was gone."

"Okay," Jesse said. "Thanks for your help. If you want to wait around while I talk with Sid you can sit in my car with Officer Cox."

"Okay."

Sid came over and told Jesse essentially the same story. He pumped up his part in it a little, telling Jesse that "we found the dead guy" but most witnesses aggrandize a little, Jesse knew.

When the boys were gone, Jesse stood in the rain with Peter Perkins while the EMTs bundled the body into the back of the ambulance.

"No flashers," Jesse said to the EMTs. "No sirens. There's no hurry."

"You going to talk with his wife?" Perkins said.

"Soon," Jesse said. "Give her a little time."

"Kids tell you anything?"

"There was a red Saab sedan, a ninety-five the kid told me, with custom wheels, that was parked by the driveway and left after the kids discovered the body."

"They didn't get any kind of license number?"

"No one ever gets a license number," Jesse said.

"I know."

"But here's what we're going to do," Jesse said. "You remember that we got a list of all the license numbers of cars parked around the woman shot in the mall parking lot."

"Yeah," Perkins said. "Sixty-seven cars."

"We're going to go through that list and see how many, if any, were red Saab sedans."

"Half the yuppies in Massachusetts drive red Saabs," Perkins said.

"So right away we cut the suspect list in half."

"Kid didn't see who was in the car," Perkins said.

"No."

"Staties come up with a list of twenty-two gun owners yet?"

"Not yet," Jesse said.

"When they do we could cross-reference that with the car list."

"We could," Jesse said.

"I can get on it after I do my shift tomorrow."

"You can get on it first thing," Jesse said. "I'll have somebody else pull your shift."

"That's gonna really squeeze us," Perkins said. "Suit and Molly are already off the roster."

Jesse looked at Perkins silently for a moment, then he said, "That would not be your worry."

"No," Perkins said. "No, 'course not."

22

"You think we cut it a little close?" he said.

"That's what makes it work for us," she said. "I lose the feeling if we don't stay close to the edge."

"I know," he said.

They were silent for a moment, holding hands, on the couch, with a pitcher of martinis.

"As long as we keep control," he said. "It was difficult to stop touching when those kids showed up."

"But we did it," she said.

"Yes," he said. "I thought about killing them too."

She shook her head emphatically.

"No," she said. "We're not doing random slaughter. That

would be like a gang bang, you know? Where's the love in a gang bang."

"I know," he said. "I'm just telling you how I nearly lost control."

"Of course, I always nearly lose control. But that's part of it, to give ourselves to it, to let it possess us entirely, and then, at the very verge of the abyss, assert our will."

He sipped his martini.

"It's sort of like this," he said. "Martinis. You like them so much you want to drink a dozen, but if you do . . ."

"The precise joy of a perfect martini is gone. You might as well slug gin from the bottle," she said.

"So we shouldn't hurry," he said.

"No, but we can start focusing in on the next one."

He leaned over and kissed her gently on the mouth.

"Let's go to the videotape," he said.

23

The three killings in an affluent suburban town led the local newscasts. The Boston papers gave it front-page coverage. Reporters and camera people hung around outside the police station. Jesse was interviewed twice, to little avail. And his picture was on the front page of the *Globe* one morning. When he came into the station on a bright Tuesday morning, Arthur Angstrom was at the desk.

"Manny, Moe, and Larry are waiting for you," Arthur said. "In the conference room."

"Perfect," Jesse said.

When Jesse went into the conference room the three

town selectmen were sitting at one end of the small conference table. Jesse pushed a pizza box aside and sat in the
fourth chair and waited.

Morris Comden cleared his throat. He was the chief selectman.

"Good morning, Jesse."

"Morris."

"You've been busy," Comden said.

Jesse nodded. The other selectmen were new to the office.
Jesse knew that Comden spoke for them.

"We just thought, Jim and Carter and I, that we probably ought to get up to speed on things."

Comden had a sharp face and wore bow ties.

Jesse nodded again. Comden smiled and glanced at the
other two selectmen.

"I told you he wasn't a talker," Comden said to the other
selectmen.

Carter Hanson had a dark tan, and silver hair combed
straight back and carefully gelled in place. He was the CEO
of a software company out on Route 128. He decided to
take charge.

He looked straight at Jesse and said, "So what's going on?"

"Three people have been killed by the same weapons,"
Jesse said. "We can find no connection among them and we
don't have any idea who did it."

"We need more than that," Hanson said.

"We do," Jesse said.

"Well, let's hear it," Hanson said.

Comden shook his head slightly and Jim Burns, the third selectman, looked uncomfortable. Jesse looked without expression at Hanson for a long moment.

"There's nothing to hear," he said.

"That's all you know?" Hanson said.

"Correct."

"You don't have any clues? Nothing?"

"Correct."

"Well, Jesus Christ," Hanson said.

Jesse nodded.

"Well," Hanson said. "What do we tell the press."

"I like *no comment*," Jesse said.

Morris Comden had a yellow legal pad in front of him. He looked down at it.

"Your department is costing a lot of overtime," he said.

Jesse nodded.

"Perhaps you could allocate your personnel a little better," Comden said.

He spoke more carefully than Hanson.

Jesse didn't say anything. Burns spoke for the first time.

"Jesus, don't you talk?" he said.

"Only when I have something to say."

"Well, maybe you could stop this undercover drug thing you've got going at the high school. We got a damn killer on the loose."

"Nope."

"For crissake, who cares if there's a couple kids smoking dope in the boys' room," Hanson said. "Where are your priorities."

"I'm a cop," Jesse said. "I been a cop for fifteen, sixteen years now. I'm good at it. I know how to do it. You don't."

"So we just stand aside and let you do what you want?"

"Exactly," Jesse said.

"Jesse," Morris Comden said. "I know how you don't like being pushed. But, for God's sake, you work for us. We have to justify your budget every year at town meeting. We have the right to know what's going on."

"I've told you what I know about the killings," Jesse said. "The undercover thing at the high school is just that, undercover."

"You won't even tell us?"

"No."

"And you won't put the personnel working the high school on the killings."

"No."

"Goddamnit," Hanson said. "We can fire you."

"You can," Jesse said. "But you can't tell me what to do."

No one said anything for a time. Comden looked down at his yellow pad and drummed the eraser end of a pencil softly on the tabletop.

Finally Comden said, "Well, I think Jim and Carter and I need to discuss this among ourselves. We'll let things ride as they are while we do."

Jesse nodded and stood up.

"Have a nice day," he said and left the room.

24

Jesse walked around his apartment. Living room, dining area, bedroom, kitchen, and bath. Through the sliding doors to his balcony he could see the harbor. Over the bar, in the corner of his living room, he could look at his picture of Ozzie Smith. On his bedside table, he could look at his picture of Jenn, in a big hat, holding a glass of wine. He walked around the apartment again. There wasn't anything else to look at. He sat on the edge of his bed for a time looking at Jenn. Then he got up and walked into the living room and stood and looked at the harbor. The apartment was so still he could hear himself breathing. He turned and went to the kitchen and got some ice and soda. He took it to the bar and made himself a tall scotch and soda with a lot of ice and sat at the bar and sipped it. There was nothing like the first one. The feeling of the first one, Jesse sometimes thought, was worth the trouble that ensued. He let the feel of the drink ease through him. Better.

He wasn't as alone as he felt, Jesse knew: Marcy, the other cops, Jenn, sort of. But that was just reasonable. In the center of himself he felt alone. No one knew him. Even Jenn, though Jenn came close. His cops were good small-town cops. But a serial killer? No one else but him was going to catch the serial killer. No one else was going to protect Candace Pennington. No one else was going to fix it with Jenn. What if he couldn't? His glass was empty. He filled it with ice and made another drink. What if the serial killer just kept killing people? He looked at the lucent gold color of his drink, the small bubbles rising through it. It looked like that odd golden ginger ale that his father had liked and no one else could stand. He could feel the pleasure of the scotch easing along the nerve paths. He felt its settled comfort in his stomach. Maybe he should walk away from it. *Maybe I should just say fuck it and be a drunk,* Jesse thought. *God knows I'm good at it.* It would certainly resolve things with Jenn.

He made a third drink.

If the killings weren't random, they were certainly connected in a way only the killer or killers understood. Which from Jesse's point of view was the same as random. He swallowed some scotch. *I feel sorry for people,* he thought, *who have never had this feeling.* So far they seemed to have killed only in Paradise. And the killings weren't random in the sense that the victims were merely those available at the moment. The woman in the mall parking lot could have been merely in the wrong place at the wrong time. But the murder at night on the beach, and the one down the dark tracks at the edge of the not yet lighted church parking lot were unlikely to be of the moment. Those victims probably had been preselected. Or the site had been. It was unlikely that the killer/killers were merely hanging around there. Say the killers had preselected the site. How did they know someone would come along for them to shoot? And how did they know that if they hung around in such unlikely places for long, someone might not get suspicious and a cop might not sooner or later show up and say whaddya doing. No, the least unlikely hypothesis was that he/they had preselected the victim and followed the victim to the site. *Elementary, my dear Ozzie.* Now that he knew that, what did he know?

Nothing.

He held the glass up and looked at the light shining through it. He wondered if Ozzie Smith had been a drinker. Probably not. Hard to do what Ozzie had done with a hangover.

The bastards weren't going to ruin that girl's life, though. If he did no other thing he was going to save Candace Pennington. He wasn't clear yet how he was going to do that, but as the alcohol worked its happy way, he knew that he could, and that he would, no matter what else.

Be good to save something.

25

At 8:10 in the morning, **Bo Marino** sat alone in the back of the school bus with his feet up on the seat next to him, smoking a joint. The smell of weed slowly filled the bus and several kids turned to look and a couple of them giggled. Bo took a deep drag and let it out slowly toward the front of the bus. The driver was a woman. Bo wondered if she even knew what pot was when she smelled it. Bo looked older than he was. He was already shaving regularly. He had been lifting weights since junior high, and it showed. His neck was short and thick, and his upper body was muscular. He was the tailback in the USC-style offense that Coach Zambello used. Several small colleges had re-cruited him, and he was very pleased with himself.

In the rearview mirror, Molly could see Bo smoking. She smelled the marijuana. *Well, well,* she thought, *Bo Marino appears to be breaking the law.* She called Jesse on her cell phone and spoke softly.

"One of the three young men we're interested in is inhal-ing a controlled substance in the back of the bus," Molly said.

Jesse was silent for a moment.

Then he said, "When you get to school, arrest him. I'll have Suit meet the bus."

"Okeydokey," Molly said.

"Aren't you supposed to say something like 'roger that,'" Jesse said.

"I like okeydokey," Molly said, and smiled and shut off the phone.

The bus pulled into the circular driveway in front of the high school and the kids got off. Bo stayed until last, smok-ing his joint, and pinched it out when there was no one else on the bus. He dropped the roach in his shirt pocket, swung his feet contemptuously off the seat, and stood.

As he got off the bus, the lady bus driver said, "Hold it there for a minute, Bo."

He stared at her.

"Hold what?" he said.

The lady bus driver took a badge out of her purse and showed it to him.

"I observed you using a controlled substance," Molly said. "We'd like you to come down to the station."

Bo stared at her. Peripherally he saw the janitor that everybody knew was a cop walking toward the bus.

"A what?"

"A controlled substance. You were observed smoking a joint on the bus. The snipe is still in your shirt pocket."

"You're fucking crazy," Bo said.

"We can go in my car," Molly said. "It's parked over here."

"Fuck you, lady," Bo said.

He started to walk past her. Molly stepped in his way.

"Don't make me arrest you," Molly said.

"You?" Bo said. "Get out of my way or I'll fuck you."

He tried to move past her again, and again Molly blocked him. Bo covered her left breast with his right hand and shoved her out of the way. Molly took a canister from her purse and sprayed him in the face. Bo made a sound that might have been a scream and clasped his hands to his face.

"Ow," he said. "Jesus Christ, ow, ow! You fucking blinded me."

Molly put the Mace away, took her handcuffs and snapped a cuff on Bo's left wrist. Suit came around the front of the bus in his janitor's outfit and pulled Bo's right hand down, and together they cuffed him.

Red-eyed, coughing, and head down, Bo was dragged into Jesse's office and put in a chair.

"My eyes are killing me," he said. "I need something for my eyes. The bitch sprayed me for no reason. Gimme something for my eyes. My father's gonna sue your ass."

"Uncuff him," Jesse said. "And leave him with me."

Molly took the cuffs off and put them in her purse. Bo immediately began to rub his eyes.

"It'll stop in a while," Jesse said. "Rubbing them won't help. We'll go down and wash them."

Molly put a bag on Jesse's desk.

"When we arrested him," Simpson said, "naturally, we patted him down for concealed weapons. Found this in his backpack."

Bo stopped coughing just long enough to say, "That's not mine, the bastards planted that."

"Be my guess that there's enough here," Molly said, "to support possession with intent."

"Wouldn't be surprised," Jesse said. "Anything else?"

"No weapon," Simpson said. "But we didn't look at everything."

Simpson put Bo's backpack on top of the file cabinet next to the window behind Jesse's desk.

"You guys may as well go back to what you were doing," Jesse said.

"Cover's pretty well blown," Molly said.

"Stay on it anyway," Jesse said.

"I never had any cover to start with," Simpson said.

Molly and Simpson went out. Jesse sat quietly looking at Bo.

"I need something for my eyes," Bo said between coughs. "I need a doctor."

Jesse didn't say anything for a while. Then he stood.

"Okay, let's go wash you off," he said.

Rinsed and dried, Bo was still red-eyed and puffy-looking, and he still coughed sporadically.

"You call my father?" Bo said.

"We're working on it," Jesse said. "Right now we got you on possession of a controlled substance with intent to sell, failure to obey a lawful command, threatening a police officer, assaulting a police officer, and being a general major-league fucking jerk."

"That bitch can't get away with spraying me like that," Bo said.

Jesse smiled. He didn't say anything. Bo sat in the chair across the desk staring hard at Jesse.

"So you gonna arrest me?" he said. "Or what?"

Jesse didn't answer him. Bo stood up.

"Fuck this," he said. "I'm walking out of here."

"Nope," Jesse said.

"You think you can stop me?" Bo said.

Jesse laughed. "Of course I can stop you," he said. "For crissake a hundred-and-twenty-pound woman hauled you in here in handcuffs."

"If you weren't a cop . . ."

"But I am a cop," Jesse said. "Sit down."

Jesse's voice was still pleasant, but there was a sudden undertone in it that made Bo uncomfortable. He didn't want to sit down. He tried looking hard at Jesse. If Jesse noticed, it didn't show. Bo sat down. Jesse picked up the backpack and put it on the desk in front of him and dumped it out. He looked at what he had. A notebook, three ballpoint pens, some Kleenex, a packet of condoms, a ruler, a protractor, two packs of spearmint gum, and a white envelope. He opened the envelope and found four prints of Candace Pennington, lying naked on the ground. *Bingo!* Her face was distorted by crying, someone out of the picture was holding her ankles, and Kevin Feeney was holding her wrists. Feeney was smiling. Jesse looked carefully at each print, then he put them faceup on his desk, facing toward Bo, and smiled at him and waited. Bo didn't look at the pictures. Jesse let the silence thicken.

Then he said, "Who's the young lady?"

"I don't know," Bo said. "I found them pictures."

"And the young gentleman?"

"I told you, I dunno. I found them."

"Where?"

"In the school library, somebody musta dropped them."

"The young lady looks like she's crying," Jesse said.

"You know how broads are, sometimes they cry after you fuck them."

"Really? And it seems that the young gentleman is restraining her."

"I don't know," Bo said.

"You don't know what?"

"I don't know nothing about that picture."

Arthur Angstrom opened Jesse's door.

"Kid's father is here," he said.

Jesse nodded.

"He's got Abby Taylor with him," Arthur said.

"Lawyer to the rescue," Jesse said. "Send them in."

26

Joe Marino was a large self-made man in an expensive suit that was a little tight for him.

"What the hell is going on here," he said when he came into the office.

"I didn't do nothing, Dad," Bo Marino said.

"Shut up," his father said. "I'll take care of this."

Jesse smiled at Abby Taylor, who had come in with Marino. She was dark-haired and good-looking, wearing a well-fitted suit with a short skirt.

"Hello, Abby," Jesse said. "How are you."

Abby Taylor said, "I'm fine."

"Hey," Marino said. "I'm talking to you."

Jesse said, "You are."

"What the hell is going on?"

"This your son?" Jesse said.

"Yes. What do you think I'm doing here?"

"We've arrested him for possession of a controlled substance with intent to sell, with resisting a lawful order, assault on a police officer, and maybe possession of obscene photographs."

"Photographs?"

"That's just a maybe," Jesse said.

"Lemme see the photographs," Marino said.

"Nope," Jesse said.

"I got a right to confront my accuser," Marino said.

Jesse took in some air and let it out.

"Explain it to him, Abby."

"Let me see if I can help with this, Mr. Marino."

"The bitch sprayed me with Mace," Bo said.

"Shut up," Marino said.

Jesse smiled at Abby and didn't say anything.

"You can release Bo to his father," Abby said.

Jesse shook his head. "We'll hold him overnight and take him over to district court in the morning."

"Jesse," Abby said. "He's seventeen. He has no previous record. At most, in this instance, he's guilty of a few minor lapses in decorum."

"He's a tough kid," Marino said. "He stood up for himself like I always taught him. Nobody pushes me around, I told him. Don't let nobody push you around, I told him, don't take crap from nobody."

Jesse nodded pleasantly. He was leaning back in his swivel chair, one foot up on the open bottom drawer of his desk, his hands resting motionless on the desktop.

"You're looking at a fucking police brutality suit, I'm telling you that right now."

Jesse picked up the phone and spoke to Arthur at the front desk.

"Molly still here? Good. Send her in."

In a moment Molly opened the door and came in.

"This is the cop that roughed up your little boy, Mr. Marino."

Marino looked at his son and shook his head disgustedly.

"Jesus Christ," he said.

"Mr. Marino," Abby Taylor said. "It might go better if you let me talk."

"Broads," Marino said and shook his head again.

"Thank you, Officer Crane," Jesse said.

"You're welcome, Chief Stone," Molly said and turned and left the room.

"Jesse," Abby said, "are you really going to keep this boy overnight?"

"I am," Jesse said.

He turned his chair a little and looked at Bo.

"I want you to understand something," Jesse said. "You deny knowing any of the people in those pictures. We will track them down and find out if that is true. If you are lying to us, you'd be wise to say so now, with your attorney present."

"I don't know them," Bo said.

"Okay, we'll bring him over to district court first thing," Jesse said, "in case you want to be there."

"Can't you do something about this?" Marino said to Abby.

"Probably not," Abby said, looking at her watch. "Especially this late."

"This is bullshit," Marino said. "I'm telling you, make it happen."

"Theoretically that's possible," Abby said. "But in fact, at this hour, I'm not going to find a judge and argue my case and have him issue a writ, so, I'm sorry, but Bo will have to spend the night."

"Dad?"

"You little shit," Marino said to Jesse.

"I'm not little," Jesse said. "I'm just not as fat as you."

Marino gave him a long stare.

"You didn't have that badge," Marino said.

"Your kid said the same thing," Jesse said. "Now unless you want to spend the night here too, why don't you and your attorney go someplace and plan your brutality case."

"She won't be my attorney long," Marino said. "I'm going to find somebody with a pair of balls."

"By which you mean a man," Abby said.

"Okay, since you asked, yeah. A man. I never seen a broad you could count on when it was on the line."

Jesse smiled.

"You're right," he said to Marino, "she won't be your attorney long."

27

Marino had left with Abby, and Bo was in the four-cell lockup in the back of the station. It was after six and getting dark when Molly came into Jesse's office with a pizza and a six-pack of Coors. She put the pizza on the desk. She separated out two cans of beer, set them on the desk next to the pizza, and put the rest in the little refrigerator where Jesse kept spring water.

"I know you're married," Jesse said. "But maybe we could have an affair."

"I'll put you on the list," Molly said. "You think we've got the little prick?"

"Yes," Jesse said.

He picked up a slice and took a bite.

When he had swallowed, he said, "There's no real grounds for an obscenity charge. I don't think the possession with intent will stand up, but we should be able to make the case for assaulting a cop. We know he's lying about the pictures. And now, we can investigate the rape without anyone thinking that Candace squealed on them."

"Won't that require Candace to testify?"

"I don't know. If we flip one of the other kids, there might be a plea bargain and she'd never have to appear."

"Why'd you keep the kid overnight?" Molly said.

Jesse ate a bite of pizza and drank some beer.

"Because I don't like him," Jesse said.

"How was the father?"

"The tree doesn't grow too far from the apple," Jesse said.

The pizza was made with green peppers and mushrooms. Jesse's favorite. He wondered if it was a coincidence, or if Molly knew. He decided that Molly knew. Molly knew a lot.

"You want me to go get Kevin Feeney?" Molly said.

Jesse sipped some beer.

"No," he said. "Not yet. We need to make it look like we didn't know who he was and it took us a couple days to find out."

"I can't show those pictures around," Molly said.

"Get the Feeney part blown up," Jesse said. "Eliminate Candace."

"Okay."

"Show them around for a couple days, principal, guidance, a few teachers and students. When we're sure the whole school knows we're looking for Feeney because we found the pictures, then we'll pick him up. Get Suit to help you. Tell him, now that he's got a legitimate reason to be there, that he can," Jesse smiled, "abandon his disguise."

"And we don't mention Candace," Molly said.

"No."

"Ever?"

"I told her I'd keep her out of it," Jesse said.

"And you keep your word," Molly said.

"When I can," Jesse said.

"When Bo gets out," Molly said, "won't he go right to his buddies and warn them?"

"Sure," Jesse said. "But they're high school kids living at home. What are they going to do? Flee the jurisdiction?"

Molly nodded.

"Might even work for us," Molly said. "The other two creeps know we're after them, it'll make them jumpy."

"The jumpier they get," Jesse said, "the easier to flip."

"And you think you can flip them?"

"My guess?" Jesse said. "All three."

28

In a spitting snow, Jesse sat in his car with the motor running and the heater on, in the parking lot outside Channel 3. He looked at the digital clock on his dashboard. Jenn would have finished her six o'clock weather. He had the wipers on low interval and between swipes the sporadic snow collected thinly on his windshield. At 6:40 Jenn came out wearing a fake fur jacket and a cowboy hat. She was with a man Jesse didn't recognize. Jesse sat for a moment listening to his own breathing, feeling his interior self dwindle and intensify. Jenn looked up at the man and laughed and bumped her head against his shoulder. Jesse turned off the motor and got out of the car. He was aware of the gun on his hip, under his jacket. Jenn saw him.

"Jesse?" she said.

"You didn't return my calls," Jesse said. "I thought I'd catch you here."

Jenn looked at him silently for what seemed to Jesse a long time, then she said, "Jesse, this is Bob Mikkleson, our station manager."

Bob was tall and healthy-looking, with silver hair combed back carefully, and lovingly sprayed. He started to put his hand out, realized Jesse wasn't going to shake hands, and put his hand back at his side.

"I'm sorry," Jenn said, "but I'm up to here. You're on the list, I would have called you tomorrow."

Jesse nodded and moved slightly closer to Bob. He didn't know why, and he hadn't planned to. There seemed to be a force outside himself. Jenn was single; she had every right to be with Bob. Bob wasn't doing anything wrong. Jesse moved a little more toward him, as if compelled by gravity. Bob was frowning.

"What was it you called about, Jesse?" Jenn said.

"Just to talk," Jesse said.

"Well," Jenn said. "Let me call you tomorrow. Bob and I have a dinner reservation."

"Sure," Jesse said.

He was next to Bob now. *What if I shot him?* The possibility made his spirit expand. But, it would mean the end of whatever was left of Jesse and Jenn. Even if he got away with it, she could never get past it. He could feel himself contract again. The muscles in his neck and shoulders bunched. He closed his eyes for a moment and took in a long drag of winter air.

Bob said, "You're the ex-husband."

Jesse nodded.

"Are you all right?" Jenn said to him.

Jesse nodded again.

"You're some sort of police chief," Bob said. "Somewhere on the North Shore."

Jesse realized that he was so close to Bob now that their sleeves touched. He nodded.

"Well," Bob said. "It's been good talking to you, but we're already late for our reservation at 9 Park, and you know how hard they are to get."

Jesse neither moved nor spoke. He could feel Jenn watching him.

"Jesse," she said.

He didn't answer.

"Jesse," Jenn said again. "We've done a lot of work since I came here from Los Angeles."

Jesse's shoulders moved, as if he were trying to loosen them.

"Don't ruin it," Jenn said.

Bob was two or three inches taller than Jesse. His skin had the smooth blue tone of a man who shaved twice a day. As close as he was, Jesse could break Bob's nose with the first punch.

"I'll call you tomorrow," Jenn said.

Bob nodded at Jesse, and the two of them walked toward Bob's car. Jesse watched them until they drove away. Then he walked slowly to his own car and opened the door and got in. He sat in his car with the door open and one foot still outside, and put his head back against the headrest and closed his eyes and concentrated on his breathing.

29

She was driving the Saab through the narrow downtown of Paradise. He sat beside her in the front seat with a Canon digital camera, which was small enough to sit comfortably in the palm of his hand.

"Her," she said.

He photographed a copper-haired woman pushing a stroller.

"We doing a woman next?" he said.

"Even it up," she said. "We've two men and a woman."

He sang, "A boy for you and a girl for me."

She joined him.

"Can't you see how happy we will be."

They both laughed.

"How about that good-looking black woman?" he said.

"Certainly," she said. "We're not racists."

Again they laughed together. He snapped a picture of the black woman.

"Don't see many black people in Paradise," he said.

She giggled.

"If we decide on her, you'll see one less," she said.

He nodded, his eyes scanning the sidewalks.

"I want this one to be a knockout," he said.

"Your choice," she said.

He photographed a tall woman in a lavender warm-up suit.

"This is fun," he said.

She turned the car right onto a street leading to the waterfront.

"I suppose it shouldn't be fun," she said.

"You mean other people would think it was awful?"

"Yes."

He put the camera on his lap and leaned back against the seat.

"When I was in college," he said, "we had to read something in English class by some old-time guy called the Venerable Bede. I don't remember it much, but I always remember one scene. There's this big banquet hall and it's brightly lit and there's a big warm fire. Outside it's cold and dark. But inside everybody's eating and drinking and having a hell of a time. A sparrow flies into one end of the hall, out of the cold darkness, and flies through the bright warm hall and out the other end into the cold darkness again."

She glanced at him as she drove. He loved to pontificate.

"So?" she said.

"So human life is like the flight of the sparrow. Or maybe it was a swallow. I can't remember, but the point's the same."

She pulled into the little parking lot by the town landing and parked in front of the restaurant.

"We're only here for a little while," she said, "and we have the right to make the most of it."

"Some people collect postage stamps," he said. "We like to kill people."

"Is it really the same?" she said.

"After we've done it, and we're making love, and the sex is like nothing else either one of us has ever known . . . the feeling . . . wouldn't you kill for that?"

She breathed in deeply for a moment and reached over and put her hand on the inside of his thigh.

"Yes," she said.

"Me too," he said.

They sat silently for a while watching the people. A dark-haired woman in a tailored suit came out of the Gray Gull. She was carrying a briefcase and talking on a cell phone. He raised his camera and aimed.

"Her," he said.

30

"I don't know why I went there," Jesse said.

"Why did you think you were going?" Dix said.

"She wasn't returning my calls. I thought maybe I could catch her coming out and we could have a drink or something."

"Catch her," Dix said.

"You think I was trying to catch her with a guy?"

"Do you?"

Dix was wearing a black turtleneck sweater today. And gray slacks. His bald head and clean-shaven face were shiny clean. His thick hands were motionless on the arms of his swivel chair, which he had tipped back while he listened to Jesse. His fingernails looked manicured.

"I want to kill anyone she's with," Jesse said. "I feel like I'll explode if I don't."

"Because . . . ?" Dix said.

"Because I love her."

"But," Dix said, "you don't kill anyone."

Jess shrugged and smiled a little

"Because I love her," Jesse said.

"You win, you lose," Dix said. "You lose, you lose."

"Exactly. Ain't love grand."

"It might not be love," Dix said.

Jesse straightened a little in his chair.

"Do shrinks believe in love?" Jesse said.

"I do," Dix said, "loosely speaking."

"I love her," he said. "If I know nothing else, I know that."

Dix nodded.

"You accept that?" Jesse said.

"Sure," Dix said. "But almost everything human operates at more than one level."

"You think there's something else at work?"

"Don't you?"

Jesse sat for a moment, looking at the palm of his right hand, flexing the fingers.

"I imagine her with them," Jesse said. "Having sex."

"She ever tell you about it?" Dix said.

"God no," Jesse said.

"So you don't know what she's doing in fact."

"I can imagine," Jesse said.

His voice was hoarse. He cleared it. Dix was entirely still in his chair. Jesse saw that he was wearing black loafers with tassels, and no socks.

"Knowledge is power," Dix said.

Jesse stared at him. Dix's face never showed anything. Jesse folded his hands and sat back in his chair with his elbows resting on the chair arms. The room was quiet. He heard his chair squeak as he shifted in it.

"But I don't know what she's doing," Jesse said.

"So you invent it," Dix said.

"Yes," Jesse said. "I guess I do."

"How long have you been inventing her life?" Dix said.

"Always," Jesse said.

31

Suitcase Simpson sat very straight in the chair across from Jesse's desk. He was always serious when he reported. Like a kid, Jesse thought, giving a school report on Denmark.

"Bo Marino," he said, "is around school bragging about how he spent a night in jail. Troy Drake is staying clear of Bo, and Kevin Feeney hasn't been in school for the past three days."

"You try his house?" Jesse said.

"Not yet, I wanted to check with you first."

"Okay," Jesse said. "Go get him."

"What about Drake?"

"We don't know that Drake was involved," Jesse said.

"Candy said . . ."

"Candace," Jesse said. "And we didn't get any of this from her, remember?"

Simpson nodded.

"And take Molly with you," Jesse said.

"You think I can't handle this alone?"

"I've seen you handle worse than this alone, Suit. Molly has a calming effect on parents."

Simpson looked pleased for a moment, and left. Jesse picked up the phone and called Abby Taylor.

"You still representing Bo Marino?" he said when she answered.

"No."

"Old man fire you?"

"He didn't get the chance," Abby said.

"Good for you."

"File him under life's too short," Abby said. "Are you going to pursue this?"

"I am."

"I wish you well."

"You know who your replacement is?"

"No, but I'll bet he's a loudmouth," Abby said.

"No bet," Jesse said. "Want to have dinner some night?"

There was a pause. Jesse waited.

Then Abby said, "Of course I would. I have always felt bad about the way we, ah, ended."

"Gray Gull?" Jesse said. "Tonight?"

Again the pause. Again Jesse waited.

"Absolutely," Abby said. "I'll meet you there."

"Good," Jesse said and hung up.

He leaned back against his chair and looked up at the ceiling for a time.

See if I can stay sober.

30

Simpson brought **Kevin Feeney** in with his mother and father. When they were seated in Jesse's office, Simpson left and closed the door behind him. Kevin's face was pale and he swallowed often. His freckles stood out starkly.

"Kevin says he doesn't know why you arrested him," Kevin's father said.

He was a smallish man with thinning red hair and a somewhat unsuccessful mustache. Mrs. Feeney had long gray hair. Her flowered dress was large and shapeless.

"Actually," Jesse said, "we haven't arrested him. We have asked him to come in and answer some questions."

"About what," Mr. Feeney said.

His voice cracked a little. Jesse took a copy of one of the photographs from a folder and slid it across the desk. Candace's face had been blacked out.

Mr. and Mrs. Feeney looked at the picture. Kevin did not.

Mrs. Feeney said, "Oh my God, Kevin, is that you?"

Mr. Feeney continued to stare at the picture. Jesse waited quietly.

After a time Mr. Feeney said, "Who's the girl?"

Jesse didn't say anything.

Mrs. Feeney said, "Kevin?"

Kevin looked at the floor.

"Kevin," Mrs. Feeney said. "Who is that girl?"

Kevin kept looking at the floor. He shook his head.

Mrs. Feeney looked at Jesse. "Who is she? Why is her face blacked out?"

"No reason to humiliate her more than necessary," Jesse said.

"But how can we help if we don't know who she is?"

"Kevin probably knows," Jesse said.

"Goddamnit, Kevin," Mr. Feeney said. "Who is she? What's going on?"

Kevin huddled up tighter into himself and stared harder at the floor. Both parents looked at Jesse.

"What's going to happen?" Mrs. Feeney said to Jesse. "He's not a criminal, you know."

"We have a picture of him forcibly restraining a naked young woman who is crying," Jesse said. "There's probably a crime in there someplace."

"How can you tell she's crying," Mrs. Feeney said.

"I've seen the full picture," Jesse said. "Face and all."

"I don't know what to do," Mr. Feeney said. "Should I get a lawyer."

"You won't need one until we arrest him," Jesse said.

"Arrest?" Mrs. Feeney said. "How can you arrest him? He's a child, for God's sake."

Jesse got up and walked around his desk and sat on the corner of it in front of Kevin.

"Who took the picture?" Jesse said.

Kevin stared at the floor.

"Did you rape this girl?" Jesse said.

Without raising his eyes, Kevin said, "I didn't do nothing."

Jesse let out an audible breath.

"This isn't skipping school, Kevin, or smoking a joint," he said. "This is jail time."

"Oh my God," Mrs. Feeney said. "Oh my God."

"I say there are three of you," Jesse said. "You holding her hands, somebody else taking the picture, and a third party, off camera, holding her feet."

"I didn't do nothing."

"Do you know Bo Marino?" Jesse said.

Kevin nodded. He looked as if he might collapse in his chair.

"Did he take these pictures?"

"I don't know."

"We found them in his possession."

"I don't know."

"Was someone holding her feet?"

"I don't know."

"Who was holding her feet."

Kevin began to cry.

"I don't know," he said. "I don't know anything."

"Don't yell at him," Mrs. Feeney said. "Leave him alone."

Jesse nodded slowly.

"Okay," he said. "Kevin Feeney, you are under arrest for sexual assault."

"No," Mr. Feeney said.

"You have the right to remain silent," Jesse said. "Anything you say can be used against you in a court of law."

"Wait a minute," Mr. Feeney said. "Wait."

"You have the right to an attorney to assist you prior to questioning and to be with you during questioning if you so desire."

"Don't arrest him," Mrs. Feeney said.

"There must be something we can work out," Mr. Feeney said.

"If you cannot afford an attorney you have the right to have one appointed for you prior to questioning."

"I don't know a lawyer," Mr. Feeney said.

"One will be appointed," Jesse said. "Do you understand these rights, Kevin?"

Kevin was crying noisily.

"Am I going to jail," he said.

"At least until a judge sets bail," Jesse said.

"Mom," Kevin said.

"Oh God, Kevin," she said.

"If he tells you?" Mr. Feeney said.

"I might not arrest him."

"Tell him, Kevin."

"I can't rat out my friends."

"Do you want to go to jail?" Mr. Feeney said. "Tell him, for crissake."

"They'll be pissed at me," Kevin said.

He was able to speak briefly, between sobs. Jesse picked up the phone.

"Molly, you or Suit come back here."

Almost at once, Simpson opened the door.

"Take Kevin down to a cell and lock him up," Jesse said. "Then call the public defender's office, tell him the kid needs a lawyer."

Simpson put a hand under Kevin's arm.

He said, "Come on, kid."

Kevin was crying loudly. Mrs. Feeney was crying just as loudly. Kevin's father stood and leaned over his son.

"Was it Bo Marino?" he shouted at him.

"Yes," Kevin said.

Simpson paused and looked at Jesse. Jesse made a wait-a-minute gesture.

"Who else," his father shouted at him.

"Troy."

"Troy Drake?"

"Yes."

"Maybe you'll sleep at home tonight," Jesse said.

33

Kevin had stopped crying. He was drinking a Coke.

Jesse said, "Who's the girl, Kevin?"

"Candy Pennington," Kevin said. "You'd have found out anyway."

"What happened?" Jesse said.

Kevin looked at his mother. No one said anything.

"It was Bo, really," Kevin said. "Me and Troy just went along."

Jesse nodded and waited. Kevin looked around. No one said anything.

"She was such a freakin' brownnose," Kevin said.

"Kevin!" his mother said.

He didn't look at her.

"Well, she was," he said. "She was always sucking up to the teachers. Always acting like she was better than anyone else."

Jesse waited. Kevin drank his Coke and didn't say anything more. The room was still.

"So you thought you'd take her down a peg," Jesse said.

"Yeah. Exactly. Bo said we should take her out in the woods and pull her pants down."

"Oh, Kevin," his mother said.

"Embarrass her, you know. Maybe take a picture of her."

Mr. Feeney had his head tilted back against his chair. His eyes were closed.

"My God, Kevin," Mrs. Feeney said.

"You're not helping, Mrs. Feeney," Jesse said. "Let him tell his story."

Mrs. Feeney clenched her hands together and pressed them against her mouth. Kevin wouldn't look at her.

"Bo told her a bunch of us were hanging out there, partying, you know. So she goes out there with us and we, you know, did it."

"What was 'it'?" Jesse said.

Mrs. Feeney made a little moaning sound into her clenched hands.

"You know, had sex. I mean we wasn't going to, we was going to just, like, look at her. But then Bo said we'd gone this far and what the hell. And then he got on top of her."

"And had sex with her?"

"Yeah."

"And you?"

"Yeah, I went second."

Mrs. Feeney moaned again. She was rocking slowly in her chair. Mr. Feeney neither moved nor opened his eyes.

"And Troy Drake?" Jesse said.

"He went after me."

"He had sex with her?"

"Yes."

"And how did she feel about this?" Jesse said.

Kevin shrugged.

"I don't know," he said.

"How did she act," Jesse said.

"She was crying," Kevin said. "When Bo did it she tried to push him off, but she couldn't."

"Did she say no?"

"I guess so, she was yelling help and stuff."

"And with you?" Jesse said.

"She just laid there," Kevin said.

"Was she still crying?"

"Yes, but that's all. It was like she decided to go along with it."

"She have any other options?" Jesse said.

"I don't know."

"So then what happened?"

"Troy did her. Then we held her down while Bo took her picture. Bo told her if she said anything we'd show everybody in school the pictures."

Mrs. Feeney continued to moan and rock. Mr. Feeney

continued to sit immobile with his head back and his eyes closed.

"I'm really sorry," Kevin said. "Mom, I am. I'm sorry."

"I tried," Mrs. Feeney said into her clenched hands. "I tried and tried to teach you to respect women. Didn't I? Didn't I drum that into you since you were little. To disrespect one woman is to disrespect us all. In shaming that poor girl, you shamed me."

Mr. Feeney opened his eyes, and without lifting it, he turned his head toward his wife.

"You know, Mira," he said. "This really is much more about Kevin and that poor girl than it is about you."

"Oh, God," Mrs. Feeney said and pressed her hands to her face again and began to cry.

Jesse reached over and shut off the tape recorder.

"I'm going to have that transcribed," Jesse said. "Then I will ask you to sign it."

"Okay."

"Mr. Feeney, you'll need to sign it too, I think, since Kevin is not of age."

Feeney nodded.

"If he testifies against the other boys," Mr. Feeney said, "can he get a break?"

"When you have a lawyer," Jesse said, "your lawyer and the DA can negotiate that."

"Will you put in a word for him?"

"Yes."

"He's never been in trouble before," Mrs. Feeney said.

"And now he is," Jesse said.

"But he won't have to go to jail?"

"Mrs. Feeney," Jesse said. "He participated in the gang rape of a sixteen-year-old girl. He'll have to answer for that."

"Oh, my God," she said and cried harder.

34

Jesse's condo was only a block away from the Gray Gull, and they walked to it after dinner. There was a hard wind off the harbor and Abby put her arm through Jesse's and pressed against him. Inside the condo Jesse poured them each a Poire Williams and they stood at the glass slider and looked out past his deck at the dark harbor. There was a storm coming up from the southwest and the water was restless.

Abby turned so that she could look up into Jesse's face. She had drunk two Rob Roys before dinner, and they had shared a bottle of Sauvignon Blanc.

"You look tired, Jesse."

"Busy time at the office," Jesse said.

"I know," Abby said. "How many television interviews have you done?"

"Many."

"And you always say it's an ongoing investigation and you can't discuss it."

"I know."

"I suppose they have to keep asking."

"It's sort of news manufacturing," Jesse said. "They do a stand-up in front of the police station and interview me, and ask me things like, have you caught the killer. And I say no. And they say, this is Tony Baloney live in Paradise, now back to you, Harry."

Abby smiled.

"It's not quite that bad," she said.

"I suppose not," Jesse said. "Sometimes they just ask if there are any developments."

"Are there?"

"Sure. We know that there were two twenty-two-caliber guns involved."

"Two?"

"Un-huh. And we think he, she, or they drives a Saab sedan. And we speculate that he, she, or they lives in Paradise."

"That's all?"

"That's all."

"Any connection among the victims?"

"Not that we can find."

"You think the killings are random?"

"Don't know. For all we know, he, she, or they had a reason to kill one of the victims, and killed the others just to make us think it was random."

"If that were the case," Abby said, "maybe the killings have stopped."

Jesse shrugged.

"Do you have a guess?"

"I try not to," Jesse said.

"Sure, but you're not just a cop," Abby said. "You are, after all, also a person."

"I'm better at being a cop. And it's best if cops don't hope."

Abby was quiet for a moment. There was a break in the cloud cover and the moonlight shone briefly on the harbor, where the whitecaps were breaking, and the boats tossed at mooring. She sipped a little of the pear brandy. It was so intense that it seemed to evaporate on her tongue.

"I'm not so sure," Abby said after a time, "that you're a better cop than a person."

"Lousy cop too?" Jesse said.

"No. You know that's not what I meant."

"I know," Jesse said. "Thank you."

They looked quietly at the foreboding whitecaps.

"I don't feel good about breaking up with you the way I did," Abby said.

"You needed to break up with me," Jesse said. "I am not really available to anyone until I resolve all this with Jenn."

"I know, but my timing wasn't good. You were in trouble and I . . ." Abby made a fluttery motion with her hand.

"It's okay, Abby."

She turned toward him and put her face up.

"It wasn't okay," she said and kissed him hard with her mouth open.

From a great distance, his ironic nonparticipant self smiled and thought *whoops!* He kissed her back.

In bed she was urgent, and when the urgency had passed for both of them, they lay side by side on their backs.

"Now it's okay," Abby said softly.

"A proper good-bye?" Jesse said.

"I suppose so."

"You're still living with that guy?" Jesse said.

"Yes . . . he's out of town tonight. Chicago."

"You thinking of marrying him?"

"Yes."

"You love him?"

"Oh God, Jesse, you're such a fucking romantic."

"I'll take that as a no," Jesse said.

"He's a nice guy."

"You're marrying him because he's a nice guy?"

"I'm marrying him because my clock is ticking fast, and he's the nicest guy I have found who wants to marry me."

"You're a practical person," Jesse said.

The overhead light was on in the bedroom, and as Jesse looked at her naked body, he could see still a faint trace of sweat between her breasts.

"Most women are," Abby said. "I always get a laugh out

of the popular mythology about romantic women and practical men."

Jesse nodded.

"It is sort of laughable," he said. "Would it bother him if he knew?"

"Of course. But he's no virgin and neither am I and we both know it."

"Do you feel like you're cheating on him?"

"Yes, I guess so, a little."

"But . . ."

"But you and I needed to be put to rest."

"And this was it?"

Abby rolled onto her side and pressed her face against Jesse's chest.

"Yes," she said. "This was it."

Jesse smiled and laughed softly.

"What?" Abby said.

"I'm the other guy," Jesse said. "The one I want to kill when Jenn is with him."

"Irony," Abby said. "You've always been a real bear for irony."

When she was dressed and her makeup was fixed and her hair was in order, Jesse offered to walk her to her car.

"I'm right in front of the Gray Gull," Abby said, "and besides, it seems righter, somehow, if I kiss you good-bye here and go out the door."

"Sure," Jesse said.

They kissed, and when they were through, Abby turned and went out the front door without a word.

There were only a few cars in the parking lot. Abby was grateful to get into her car and out of the wind. She started the engine and put it in gear and drove out of the lot. A red Saab sedan pulled out of the lot behind her. Both cars turned down Front Street.

35

She had been shot twice in the chest, as she got out of
her car, in the driveway of her house on North Side Drive,
her body turned toward the back of the car, as if she had
turned to see what was behind her. Anthony deAngelo
had found her on routine patrol. She had fallen with the car
door open, and one foot still caught on the edge of the car.
Anthony had seen the car with its interior lights on and
stopped to take a look.

"It's Abby Taylor," deAngelo said to Jesse when he
arrived.

Jesse nodded. *Dead people don't look much different at first,* he thought. *Just like live people except that they don't move.* He stared down at her face. *No,* he thought, *it's more than that. You look at them, there's something missing.* Her position would have embarrassed her. He reached down and moved her leg and smoothed her skirt down. She was still flexible. Peter Perkins arrived with his crime-scene kit. Suitcase Simpson was setting up lights. The ambulance pulled in. Anthony was stringing the crime-scene tape.

"She live alone?" Suitcase asked.

"She lived with a guy," Jesse said.

He was still looking absently down at the body.

"Nobody answering the door," Simpson said. "Or the phone."

"He's in Chicago," Jesse said.

Simpson stared at Jesse and started to speak. Then he didn't. One of the techs from the ambulance came over and knelt down beside Abby. He took her pulse automatically, though he knew she was dead.

"Just like the other ones, Jesse," the tech said. "Two in the chest."

"Her purse is still in the car," Perkins said.

"Cold night," the tech said. "Make time of death a little harder."

"She died within the last hour," Jesse said.

The tech looked up as if he were going to ask a question. Suitcase Simpson put a hand on his shoulder. The tech glanced at him. Simpson shook his head. Perkins began to photograph the crime scene. A few neighbors had straggled out into the cold, coats on over sleepwear, hunched against the cold, staring aimlessly. Jesse was motionless, looking down at the body.

"You know where this guy might be in Chicago," Simpson asked.

Jesse shook his head.

"Anthony and I'll ask a few neighbors," Simpson said. "Maybe they'll know. Or know where he works and the people at work will know."

Jesse nodded.

"Hate to just leave a note for him to call."

"We won't leave a note," Jesse said. "If you can't reach him, leave somebody here until you do."

"What if it's a couple days?" Simpson said.

"Leave somebody here if you can't reach him," Jesse said.

"Okay, Jesse."

The other cops went about their crime-scene business very quietly. Like people in a sickroom. Jesse continued to look at Abby. After a while the EMTs loaded her onto a gurney and slid her into the back of the ambulance. Jesse watched them silently. The ambulance pulled away. Peter Perkins packed up his crime-scene gear and went to his car. Simpson and deAngelo finished talking to the neighbors.

"They told me he works at the GE in Lynn," Simpson said. "I'll call them in the morning. Anthony says he'll stay here. I'll get Eddie to come over in the morning and give him a break."

"Do that," Jesse said.

Perkins got into his truck and drove away. DeAngelo settled in behind the wheel in his cruiser in front of the house.

"I gotta get going, Jesse," Simpson said.

Jesse nodded. Simpson shifted his weight a little.

"You, ah, gonna be all right?" he said.

"Yes."

"Okay," Simpson said.

He walked back toward his cruiser. And stopped and turned back toward Jesse.

"I'm sorry about Abby," he said.

"Thanks, Suit."

Simpson got into his cruiser, started it, and drove down North Side Drive. In the rearview mirror he could see that Jesse was still standing where he'd left him.

36

The Paradise selectmen called a special town meeting, which authorized a $10,000 reward for information leading to the arrest of the killer or killers. A telephone hot line was established and the number publicized statewide. The Paradise police were working twelve-hour shifts, and the hot line was manned in the town clerk's office by off-duty firemen. A meeting room in the Paradise Town Hall had been converted to a press headquarters. Vans from the Boston television stations were parked in the public works lot behind the town hall, and almost every day a television reporter was doing a live report standing in front of the Paradise Police Station.

Police in Paradise are pressing their search today for the killer or killers in a series of seemingly random murders that have terrorized this affluent North Shore community. In a news conference earlier today, Paradise Police Chief Jesse Stone said the full resources of his department, augmented by the Massachusetts State Police are being brought to bear on this investigation. But to this point the reign of terror continues. Reporting live in Paradise, this is Katy Morton. Back to you, Larry.

That's a tense situation up there, Katy. Now to other news, an heroic Siamese cat today . . .

Jesse shut off the television. With him in his office was a state police sergeant named Vargas.

"Jeez," he said. "Didn't you want to know about that cat?"

"I've got enough excitement in my life," Jesse said. "How many people can you give me?"

"Captain says we'll continue to help with the investigation, and he wants to know what else you need. How many patrols you got out now?"

"Five cars, two shifts."

"Ten people," Vargas said. "How many people you got on the force?"

"Twelve," Jesse said. "Including me. Molly Crane covers the desk days, and I stay here at night."

"You're swamped," Vargas said. "I'll get some of our guys to cover the night patrols. Captain says to tell you that we aren't taking this thing over. You're still in charge of it. I'm just liaison."

"You'll need an office, and a phone," Jesse said. "You can set up in the squad room."

Molly came into the office without knocking. She was holding a business card. Her eyes looked heavy. She put the card on Jesse's desk.

"There's a reporter from one of those national talk shows," Molly said. "Wants to interview you."

"No," Jesse said.

He didn't look at the card. Molly smiled.

"He won't like this," Molly said. "He's kind of pleased that he's famous."

"There's a press briefing every morning," Jesse said. "Tell him where and when."

Molly nodded and went out.

"Press don't like being stonewalled," Vargas said.

"Who does."

"They can say bad things about you," Vargas said.

"Who can't," Jesse said.

Vargas grinned.

"Don't seem too media savvy," he said.

"My people are beginning to sag," Jesse said. "How soon can we get some patrol help?"

"Tonight," Vargas said.

"Good," Jesse said. "How close is Healy to getting me a list of people who've bought twenty-two firearms or ammo?"

"I'll check," Vargas said. "Those records aren't always immaculate, and even if they were, people get guns from a lot of places."

"I need whatever he's got," Jesse said.

Molly stuck her head in the door again.

"Jenn," she said, "on line one. You want to take it?"

Jesse nodded.

"Sit tight," he said to Vargas. "I'll only be a minute."

He picked up the phone and punched line one and said, "Hi."

"Was that woman that got killed the one you used to date?"

"Yes."

"Oh, Jesse, I'm so sorry."

"Thank you," Jesse said. "What's up?"

"My news director and I had a fabulous idea," Jenn said.

Jesse closed his eyes and put his head back against his chair.

"Every news outlet in the country is dying for some sort of inside something on this," Jenn said.

"I know."

"We thought because of our, ah, connection, you know? We thought I could come out with a cameraman and track the investigation. An inside look at the workings of a police manhunt. We would stay out of your way. And when you catch the guy we'd have a whole series about it, and maybe a special, and maybe we could sell it to one of the national outlets . . ."

"No," Jesse said.

"Oh, I know, Jesse. Believe me I know what an imposition it is. But we'd stay out of the way, and, Jesse, it would mean so much to my career."

Jesse still had his eyes closed and his head back.

In a soft voice, he said, "No, Jenn," and put the phone back in its cradle.

37

Chuck Pennington was an architect. He had been an inter-
collegiate boxing champion at Harvard and still looked in
shape.

He must have been pretty good, Jesse thought. *There's not a
mark on his face.*

He had thick black hair brushed straight back. He wore
a rust-colored tweed jacket and a blue oxford shirt. He sat
with Jesse in the living room of the house he'd designed,
with his wife and daughter and a lawyer named Sheldon
Resnick. Molly Crane sat near the door. Through the glass
back wall of the living room Jesse could look a long way out
over the Atlantic Ocean. Mrs. Pennington was speaking.

"We wanted to spare you this," she said to her husband. "We know how important your work is."

"My daughter is more important than my work," Pennington said. "But we can put that aside for the moment and listen to Chief Stone."

"You promised to keep my daughter's name out of this," Mrs. Pennington said.

"I did what I promised your daughter I would do," Jesse said.

"You spoke to her without me?" Mrs. Pennington said.

"It seemed the only way I could," Jesse said.

"Sheldon," she said. "I want you to make that clear to this policeman that we will not tolerate scandal."

"Mr. Stone has been nice to me," Candace said.

"Candace, you be quiet," Mrs. Pennington said.

"No, Margaret," Pennington said. "You are the one that has to be quiet."

"Chuck . . ."

"This didn't happen to you," Pennington said. "It happened to Candace. It matters what Candace wants."

"My God, Chuck, she's . . ."

Resnick put his hand on Mrs. Pennington's forearm.

"Chuck's right, Margaret. Now is not the time."

Mrs. Pennington opened her mouth, then closed it, and clamped her lips and sat back in her chair and folded her arms.

Pennington turned in his chair and looked at Jesse. He had very pale blue eyes.

"I know the kind of pressure you must be under now," he said. "And I appreciate your taking the time for this."

"Candace has always known who raped her," Jesse said. "But she and I agreed that if she blew the whistle on them, uncorroborated, we might not get them, and her life in Paradise would be ruined."

Pennington nodded.

"They were going to show my picture to everyone," Candace said.

Pennington nodded again. He showed no emotion, though Jesse noted that the knuckles on his clasped hands looked white.

"Now they probably won't," he said.

He looked at Jesse.

"No," Jesse said. "They won't. They're scared."

"Good," Candace said.

Jesse nodded slowly.

"And they're scared of you," Jesse said.

Candace looked at Jesse, then at her father, and then, more covertly, at her mother.

"Excellent," she said.

"The law always talks about justice," Jesse said. "We're officially in favor of it. But if I were you what I would want would be revenge."

"Chief Stone . . ." Mrs. Pennington said.

Her husband shook his head at her.

"That's what I would like," he said.

"Okay," Jesse said. "Marino, Feeney and Drake have incriminated themselves. If we didn't know anything about you the pictures would have led us to you."

Candace nodded. She understood.

"So we need a statement," Jesse said. "And if we go to court we'll need you to testify."

"Will anyone else see those pictures?" Candace said.

"If we go to trial," Jesse said, "the defense will argue that you were a willing participant and made up the rape story. The pictures would be evidence to the contrary."

"My God, naked pictures of my daughter," Mrs. Pennington said. "In public. I won't permit it."

"We're a long way past propriety here, Margaret. It's Candace's decision."

"She's not old enough to decide something like this," Mrs. Pennington said.

"I'll give a statement," Candace said. "And I'll testify if I have to."

"Candace . . ."

"Good," Jesse said. "Is there someplace you can go and give Molly your statement?"

"They can use the kitchen," Pennington said.

As she followed Candace from the room, Molly smiled at Jesse, and, shielding the gesture with her body, gave him a thumbs-up. Everyone was quiet for a moment. Jesse looked through the big window at the brisk gray ocean.

"Kids like Candace," Jesse said, still looking at the ocean, "often need some therapy after an experience like this one."

"You mean from a psychiatrist?" Mrs. Pennington said.

"Yes," Jesse said. "If you need a referral I can get one for you."

Mrs. Pennington looked at her husband.

"We'll see," he said. "Thanks for the offer."

"As far as the case goes," Resnick said, after a moment, "a plea bargain would certainly seem possible."

"Be up to the defense lawyers and the DA," Jesse said.

"But you agree that it could happen?" Mrs. Pennington said.

"It often does," Jesse said.

38

"We had sex an hour before she died," Jesse said.

Dix nodded.

"I'm sad," Jesse said. "And I'm insulted."

Dix tilted his head slightly.

"I'm the chief of police and I'm trying to catch these bastards and they shoot a woman I just made love to."

"You think it was intentional?" Dix said.

"I don't know," Jesse said. "But it makes me mad."

"And you think it was more than one person?" Dix said.

"Yes. The two guns don't make any sense to me otherwise."

Dix was wearing a blue blazer today, and a white shirt. Everything about him gleamed. His shaved head, his starched shirt, his thick-soled mahogany shoes. He sat with his hands laced over his flat stomach, rubbing the tips of his thumbs together.

"Jenn called me after Abby was killed," Jesse said. "And said she hoped I was okay."

Dix waited, moving the tips of his thumbs softly back and forth.

"Then she said she wanted me to give her special access to the sniper killing, her and a cameraman, inside coverage, follow the whole investigation."

Dix nodded encouragingly

"Four people die, and she sees it as a career opportunity."

"Why would she think you'd allow that?" Dix said.

Jesse smiled without humor.

"Because she is the, ah, object of my affections," he said.

"Object?"

"Just being amusing," Jesse said.

Dix didn't say anything. They were quiet. The room shimmered with stillness. Jesse took in some air. His movements were stiff. Dix waited. He seemed perfectly comfortable waiting. Jesse's stiffness loosened.

"She said once," Jesse's voice was hoarse, "that what I really love is my fantasy of her, and I keep trying to squeeze her into it."

"What did you say?"

"I said it was fucking shrink talk."

Dix grinned.

"The object of your affection," Dix said.

"More fucking shrink talk," Jesse said.

Dix smiled.

"Sure," he said. "I am, after all, a fucking shrink."

39

There were too many of them for Jesse's office, so they
went to the conference room in the station. Jesse was there,
at the head of the conference table. Beside him sat an Essex
County assistant district attorney named Martin Reagan.
Molly and Suitcase Simpson stood against the wall. Bo
Marino and his parents sat on one side of the table. Troy
Drake and his mother sat on the other side. Two lawyers
from a big Boston firm representing both families sat at the
end of the table opposite Jesse. The lead attorney was a sleek
red-haired woman named Rita Fiore. The other lawyer was
a small man with a narrow face and a graying Vandyke
beard. His name was Barry Feldman.

"Here's what we got," Jesse said. "Or at least all of it I can remember. There's so much that Marty may have to remind me."

Rita smiled.

"So we begin," she said.

"We have a sworn statement from Kevin Feeney that he and Bo Marino and Troy Drake raped Candace Pennington and photographed her naked."

"I understand that he is clearly identifiable in the pictures," Rita said.

"He is," Jesse said.

"How stalwart of him to admit it," Rita said.

"We have Candace Pennington's sworn statement that Kevin Feeney, Bo Marino, and Troy Drake raped her and photographed her naked."

"Hardly a disinterested observer," Rita said.

Martin Reagan said, "Rita, let's wait until we get into court to try the case. We simply want to question the suspects, and they simply wanted their attorney present."

"Which would be me," Rita said. She glanced at Feldman beside her, "and of course Barry."

"Barry Feldman," the other lawyer said.

Jesse nodded. He looked at Troy Drake.

"You got anything you want to say, Troy?"

Troy Drake was very blond with a full-lipped sulky mouth that made him look vaguely like Carly Simon. His mother was as blond as he was, and had the same sulky mouth.

"I've advised my clients not to discuss the case," Rita said.

Feldman nodded.

"You all planning to take her advice?" Jesse said.

No one at the table spoke.

"Okay," Jesse said. "These officers will read you your rights and escort you to your cell."

"You already arrested me and I got released to my old man," Bo said.

"That was for a different crime," Jesse said. "This is a new arrest."

"Can they do this?" Mrs. Drake said.

"I'll have them out in a few hours," Rita said.

"I'm going to ask for remand," Reagan said.

"Marty, don't be ridiculous," Rita said. "These are children."

"So is Candace Pennington," Reagan said.

"They can't put my son in jail," Mrs. Drake said. "I know he didn't do anything."

Mrs. Marino was crying. Mr. Marino was red-faced.

"You better keep my kid out of jail," he said to Rita.

"Mr. Marino," Rita said. "I am the chief criminal litigator at Cone Oakes and Belding. I'm about as good as it gets. You don't frighten me. Nothing does, and it is not in your best interest to annoy me."

Marino looked startled.

"The boys may have to spend the night in jail, but we can get them in front of a judge tomorrow and get them released on bail. I am confident that I can forestall a remand."

"What's a remand," Mrs. Drake said.

"Remand to jail to await trial."

"My God, is that what's going to happen now?"

"No. It won't happen at all. But now the police will hold your son until tomorrow when we can get them before a magistrate."

"They're children. They can't have to be thrown in with the general prison population," Mrs. Drake said.

"We'll hold them here," Jesse said. "It's a four-cell lockup. They will be the general prison population."

"This is crap," Troy said.

His mother put her hand on his arm. Jesse could tell that neither Troy nor Bo Marino liked the talk about them being children.

"You got that right," Bo said. "That little wimp prick is lying."

"Please be quiet," Rita said to both boys.

"The wimp prick being Feeney?" Jesse said.

"Sure. You got him and the fucking baby says whatever you want him to, so he can get off."

"And Candace?" Jesse said.

"Bitch would say anything to get me in trouble," Troy said. "She's been hot for me since ninth grade, and I won't give her a nod."

"Is she hot for Bo, too?" Jesse said.

"Be quiet," Rita said to both boys.

"Let 'em talk, lady," Joe Marino said. "Somebody's trying to frame my kid and you're telling him not to say anything?"

"They're not doing themselves any good," Rita said.

"She hot for Bo?" Jesse said to Troy.

"I don't know. Maybe Bo did her for all I know, him and Kevin was always talking about doing this broad and that one."

"You cocksucker," Bo said.

Mrs. Marino paused in her crying long enough to say, "Bo!"

No one paid any attention.

"So maybe they did her," Troy said, "and the bitch thought when she got them she could throw me in there and get even."

"Shut up." Rita's voice was sharp in the room.

But the genie was out of the bottle.

"So why did Kevin name you as well," Jesse said.

"Fucking loser," Troy said. "He's always sucking up to Bo."

Rita's hand slammed flat on the tabletop and her voice was like a blade.

"Shut fucking up," she said.

Everyone looked at her. The room was suddenly still except for Mrs. Marino's crying. Joe Marino made a cool it gesture at his son. Mrs. Drake squeezed Troy's hand as hard as she could.

"You keep talking and you'll talk yourselves right into a mess I can't get you out of. Do you understand me?"

No one said anything. Bo and Troy looked suddenly scared.

"Good," Rita said. "You will talk to no one unless I'm present, or Barry. You will say nothing unless I say to, or Barry."

"Rita," Marty Reagan said. "This doesn't look like one for all and all for one."

"I know," Rita said.

She looked at her clients.

"What Mr. Reagan means is that I can't represent clients in circumstances where the best interest of one might collide with the best interests of the other."

Both families looked a little blank. But she had frightened them enough to make them docile.

"So," she said. "Let them stay here tonight. Tomorrow Barry or I, it will probably be Barry, will get them out on bail, and then we'll organize your legal representation."

"You can't pull out on us now," Joe Marino said.

"I can't represent both of the boys," Rita said.

"So let him represent Troy," Marino said.

"Same firm, Mr. Marino. I'll see to it that you are both well represented, but this is not the place, and now is not the time."

She turned and nodded very slightly to Jesse.

"Okay, Molly," Jesse said. "You and Suit read the words and take them down to a cell."

Mrs. Marino's crying rose to a wail. Both Bo and Troy looked as if they had trouble swallowing. Joe Marino started to argue. Mrs. Drake seemed frozen in place. Molly said the Miranda for both of them and she and Simpson took them from the room. Their parents went with them.

"Checking the accommodations," Reagan said when they were gone.

Rita Fiore said, "When are you going to arraign them, Marty?"

"You should have them there at nine A.M.," Reagan said.

"Salem?"

"Yep."

"Can you take care of that, Barry?"

Feldman nodded and made a small entry in his notebook.

"Now," Rita said. "In the event that I'm still representing someone in this cluster fuck, it seems to me like there are deals to be made."

"Let's permit the dust to settle," Reagan said, "before we start bargaining."

"Just as long as you see what I see," Rita said.

Reagan smiled, and got to his feet.

"We done here?" he said.

Jesse nodded. So did Rita.

"Barry," Rita said. "I'll be along in a little while. Why don't you get the car warmed up."

Feldman stowed the notebook in his inside pocket and stood and picked up his briefcase.

"Nice meeting you all," he said.

"I'll walk you to your car," Reagan said, and both men left.

40

Rita stood and came down the length of the table and sat on the edge of it near Jesse. Jesse understood that she was letting him get a look at her. She knew she was very good-looking.

"I did a little background research," Rita said.

"Thorough," Jesse said.

"I am very thorough," Rita said. "I also have the resources of a huge law firm."

"Fortunate," Jesse said.

Rita smiled.

"Try not to babble," she said.

"Hard," Jesse said.

Rita smiled and nodded.

"You were a homicide detective in Los Angeles," Rita said. "Captain Cronjager out there says you were very good."

Jesse nodded.

"But your marriage went south and you had a drinking problem."

Jesse nodded again.

"How's your marriage?" she said.

"South," Jesse said.

Rita smiled.

"And the drinking?"

"Better."

"My paralegal talked with the state police homicide commander," Rita said.

"Healy," Jesse said.

"Usually you get into one of these suburban towns and they have a homicide, the state police take over the investigation pretty quickly."

Jesse nodded.

"Healy says it's not the case here."

"We do as much as we can in-house," Jesse said.

"Healy says you know what you're doing."

"I do," Jesse said.

"I also know," Rita said, "like about everyone else in the damned world, that you got a serial killer operating here."

"I do."

"You must be stretched pretty thin."

"We are."

"But you had time to run this down."

Jesse nodded. He could feel the force of Rita's sexuality. All her movements, every gesture of her head, every verbal tone, was carnal. He knew it was real, and he knew she used that.

"These kids do it?" Rita said.

"Absolutely," Jesse said.

"No reasonable doubt?"

"None," Jesse said.

"Well," Rita said. "Maybe I can create one."

"Hope not," Jesse said.

Rita stood and smoothed her skirt down over her thighs.

"I just like to get a feel for the case," she said. "Healy told us you were a, what did he say? It was kind of cute. Oh, he said you were a straight shooter."

"That is cute," Jesse said.

Rita smiled and put on a coat with a big fur-trimmed hood, which she put up carefully over her hair.

"I hope we can talk again," she said.

"You know where to find me," Jesse said.

Rita looked at him thoughtfully for a moment.

"Do you want me to find you?" she said.

"I believe I do," Jesse said.

41

Healy pushed his way past the cluster of reporters outside the Paradise Police Station. One of the print reporters recognized him.

"Captain Healy," he said. "Is there a break in the sniper case?"

Microphones were pressed upon him. Television cameras came suddenly to life.

"Have the state police taken over the case? Are you planning to offer a reward . . . Is there forensic evidence . . . Why are you here . . . Do you think the Paradise police are competent to handle a case of this magnitude . . . Is the FBI involved . . . Is there a chance they will be . . . Do you have a theory of the case . . . Are you comfortable working with Chief Stone . . . ?"

Healy ignored it as if it were not there. He went in through the front door and closed it behind him. He said hello to Molly and went past her to Jesse's office.

"There are a hundred and twenty-three thousand people in this great Commonwealth," Healy said, "who have bought a twenty-two weapon, or twenty-two ammunition in the past year."

He sat down.

"Their days are numbered," Jesse said.

"Or his, or hers," Healy said.

"I think it's two people," Jesse said.

Healy was quiet for a moment, thinking about it.

"Yeah," he said. "I do too."

"How many of those hundred and twenty-three thousand live in Paradise?"

"One hundred and eighty-two," Healy said.

"And how many of them own a late-model red Saab ninety-five?"

"Three."

Jesse felt his solar plexus tighten.

"And," he said, "how many of those three Saabs were parked up at the Paradise Mall when Barbara Carey got shot."

"According to the plate numbers your people collected," Healy said, "one."

Jesse felt himself coil tighter.

"And the lucky winner is?" he said.

"Anthony Lincoln," Healy said.

He put a note card on the desk.

"Name, address, phone," Healy said. "He has no criminal record."

Jesse picked up the card and looked at it.

"He has a class-A carry permit," Healy said. "In the past year he has purchased a Marlin twenty-two rifle, model nine-nine-five, semiauto with a seven-round magazine, and two boxes of twenty-two long ammunition."

"The son of a bitch," Jesse said.

"Be useful if we could tie the rifle to the shootings," Healey said.

"Funny gun for the kind of shooting we've been seeing," Jesse said. "I'd have said handgun."

"People use the guns they can get," Healy said.

"Think we got enough to confiscate it?"

"No. All you got is he owns a twenty-two and his car was parked near one of the murders."

"And it's a Saab," Jesse said. "Like the one at the church parking lot."

Healy shrugged.

"Talk to the ADA on the case," Healy said. "Maybe he's tight with a judge."

"Even if we can't compel him," Jesse said. "Any good citizen would be willing to submit his gun for forensics testing, unless he had something to hide."

Healy smiled.

"Unless he wished to vigorously resist the intrusion of government on the individual's right to privacy," he said.

"Unless that," Jesse said. "I guess I'll go and visit him."

"You might want to be a little careful with this guy," Healy said. "If he's your man he's already killed four people."

"I'm a little careful with everyone."

"The hell you are," Healy said. "The last one killed, the Taylor woman, didn't you used to go out with her?"

"I did."

"It will not be good," Healy said, "if you take it too personal and turn into Rambo on us."

"It's the trick of being a good cop, isn't it," Jesse said. "You got to care about the victim, and you got to care about the job."

Healy nodded.

"And you got to be unemotional at the same time."

"'Course not everyone is a good cop," Healy said.

Jesse was silent for a moment, looking at the top of his desk. Then he raised his head and looked at Healy.

"I am," Jesse said.

"Good point," Healy said.

42

Anthony Lincoln's address was a condo that had been rehabbed out of an old resort hotel on the south side of Paradise, where it faced the open ocean. With Jesse in the front seat beside him, Suitcase Simpson parked the cruiser in a guest parking space off the cobblestone turnaround to the right of the entrance. A discreet sign said ONE HOUR PARKING. VIOLATORS WILL BE TOWED.

"That's welcoming," Jesse said.

The building was an overpowering display of weathered shingle architecture, punctuated with brick and brass and copper that was greening beautifully. A dark green sign, larger than it needed to be, said *SEASCAPE,* in gold-colored scroll. Simpson was in uniform. Jesse wore a leather jacket, jeans, and sneakers.

The lobby was two stories high. The floor was a gray marble. The moldings and door casings were driftwood, or something that had been processed to look like driftwood. A concierge desk stretched along one side of the lobby, and a bank of elevators faced them. The third wall of the lobby was glass, overlooking the beach and the ocean. Jesse held his badge out for the concierge to see. She looked at it carefully.

"Are you the chief?" she said.

"I am," he said. "Jesse Stone. This is Officer, ah, Luther Simpson."

"What can I do for you?" the concierge said carefully.

Hers was a job that could be lost by one indiscretion.

"Anthony Lincoln live here?" Jesse said.

"Yes sir, the penthouse unit."

"Anyone live here with him?"

The concierge was pale-skinned. Her dark hair was up. She was dressed in a dark skirt-and-blazer outfit with a small yachting crest on the blazer. She thought about the question.

"Well, Mrs. Lincoln, of course."

"And her first name is?" Jesse said.

"Ah." The concierge tapped the computer built into her desktop. "Brianna, Brianna Lincoln."

"Thank you," Jesse said. "We'll go up."

"I can call up for you, sir."

"No need," Jesse said as he and Simpson walked to the elevators.

When they got to the penthouse floor, the elevator opened into a small foyer furnished with a tan leather wing chair and a Chinese red-lacquered end table. Anthony and Brianna Lincoln were waiting for them at their door.

"Chief Stone?" Anthony said. "The concierge called ahead."

"I'm Jesse Stone," Jesse said. "This is Luther Simpson, may we come in?"

"Of course," Anthony said. "Tony Lincoln, this is my wife, Brianna."

The room was spectacular, Jesse thought. Glassed in on three sides, it overlooked the beach, the ocean, and the stretch of hard coast, where expensive houses had been built among the rocks. There was a vast white rug, blond furniture, and cream-colored full-length drapes that looked as if one could close them if one tired of the view. *Everything matches,* Jesse thought. *Everything is clean and exact and just right, and it looks like nobody lives here.* Simpson looked around uneasily.

"We'll need to talk," Jesse said. "This all right?"

"Of course," Brianna said. "Would you like some coffee?"

"Sure," Jesse said. "Cream and sugar. Suit?"

Simpson shook his head. He was still standing.

"No coffee for me," he said.

Brianna smiled and went to the kitchen.

"Why don't you sit there, Suit," Jesse said, "by the door."

Tony Lincoln was slim and tall. His hair was combed back in a neat wave, parted on the left side, and so blond that it was almost white. He had a deep tan which, Jesse thought, meant either winter vacation or tanning lamp. It balanced well with his pale hair. His eyes were very blue and his movements were alert and graceful.

"What did you call him?" Anthony said.

Brianna returned from the kitchen.

"Coffee is brewing," she said.

Jesse nodded and smiled at her. Then he answered Tony's question.

"Suit," Jesse said. "Short for Suitcase."

"Harry 'Suitcase' Simpson," Anthony said. "The baseball player."

"Exactly," Jesse said.

Tony not only knew baseball, Jesse thought, he'd remembered Suit's last name.

"Tony remembers every baseball player that ever lived," Brianna said. "And most other things, too."

Brianna was as slim as her husband and nearly as tall, with thick black hair worn short. She was as tan as Anthony, and carefully made up. Her mouth was wide and her dark eyes were very big. She was barefooted in faded jeans and a scoop-necked white T-shirt. Her husband was wearing gray suede loafers with no socks, satin sweatpants, and a V-necked black cashmere sweater. The sleeves of the sweater were pushed up over his forearms. He smiled.

"Great game," he said.

"It is," Jesse said.

"Ever play?" Tony said.

"I did," Jesse said.

"I did too," Lincoln said. "And I've never liked anything so well again."

"Well, excuse me," Brianna said.

Tony smiled.

"Except you," he said.

"You're just saying that because you want coffee," Brianna said, and got up and went again to the kitchen.

Tony laughed before he turned to Jesse.

"So what can we do for you, Jesse? Okay if I call you Jesse?"

"You bet," Jesse said. "Let's wait until Mrs. Lincoln comes back."

"Brianna," Tony said. "Tony and Brianna. We don't stand on a lot of formality here."

Jesse nodded. He smiled to himself. Suit looked very large and uncomfortable in the fancy chair by the door. Brianna came back in with coffee on a small tea wagon. Good china. Good silver.

When they had settled back with their coffee, Jesse said, "First, thanks for being so gracious. This is a routine investigation, we've cross-referenced a lot of data and now we just have to boil it down by eliminating the people we've come up with."

"Is it the killings?" Brianna said.

Even sitting across from her he could smell her perfume. *And heat,* Jesse thought. *I can almost feel heat from her.*

"Yes, ma'am, it is," Jesse said.

Jesse could see Suit, by the door out of sight of the Lincolns, staring at Jesse.

"We're trying to run down every twenty-two-caliber firearm owned by a resident of Paradise."

"Ah," Tony said and smiled. "That's it."

Jesse nodded. He took a small notebook out of his jacket pocket and opened it.

"You appear to own a twenty-two rifle," he said, reading from the notebook, "Marlin model nine-nine-five, semiauto with a seven-round magazine."

"We do," Tony said, and grinned at Jesse, "if you know that, you probably know that we have a permit."

"I do," Jesse said. "You also bought two boxes of twenty-two long ammunition for it."

"Yep, got about a box and a half left. We got a country place in the Berkshires and when we're out there we like to plink vermin."

Jesse nodded

"Do you have the gun here, Tony?" he said.

"Sure, we keep it locked up in the bedroom closet."

"May we see it?"

"Sure, Brianna? You want to get it for us?"

"Of course," she said and hurried out of the room.

Jesse admired her backside, then shifted his glance to the big picture window. The ocean looked silvery blue today with the sun shining on it.

"Great view, isn't it," Tony said.

"I assume you pay for it," Jesse said.

"Oh, boy," Tony said, "you got that right."

"What do you do for work," Jesse said.

Tony smiled.

"Mostly, these days, I manage our money," he said. "I used to be an ophthalmologist. Then one day I invented an ocular scanning device that became the standard for the profession."

He smiled again.

"Sometimes it's better to be lucky than good," he said.

"And you don't practice medicine anymore?" Jesse said.

"Why, do you have something in your eye?"

Jesse smiled.

"Just wondered."

"No, I don't practice anymore," Tony said.

"You miss it?"

"Can't say that I do."

Brianna came back into the room carrying the rifle in both hands. Jesse was aware that Simpson shifted a little in his seat by the door. Brianna gave Jesse the gun. He pointed it at the floor, released the magazine into his hand and put it on the table beside him, worked the action a couple of times, then opened the bolt and looked at the barrel.

"Nice and clean," he said.

"Good workman takes care of his tools, right, Jesse?"

Jesse nodded.

"We'd like to borrow this for a couple of days. I'll give you a receipt, and test-fire it so we can cross you off the list."

"Be pretty suspicious," Tony said, "if we didn't let you."

"It would," Jesse said.

"Could they make a mistake?" Tony said.

"No," Jesse said. "This is pretty straightforward ballistics."

"Okay with me," Tony said. "You go along with that, Brianna?"

"Certainly."

Jesse stood and handed the rifle to Simpson.

"Thanks," Jesse said. "We'll get it back to you promptly."

"That'll be fine, Jesse," Tony said.

He and Brianna were both on their feet.

"Thanks for the coffee," Jesse said.

"We enjoyed the company," Brianna said. "Good luck with the dreadful murders."

"Yes," Tony said. "And if you come up with a case of conjunctivitis, give me a call. You too, Suitcase."

They shook hands and Tony walked them to the elevator.

"I hope you get the sonovabitch," he said.

"Sooner or later," Jesse said.

The elevator door opened, Jesse and Suit got in. Jesse punched one and the door glided shut.

43

As they drove back along Atlantic Avenue, Suitcase Simpson said to Jesse, "We are cops, are we not?"

"We are."

"And there's a donut shop down here on the right past the Catholic church, is there not?"

"And you feel that in order to certify our cop-ness we have to go in there and scarf some down?"

"Yes," Simpson said. "I do."

"You're right," Jesse said. "It's been too long."

Suit swung the car into the Dunkin' Donuts parking lot. Simpson kept the car idling, while Jesse got out and went in and bought a dozen donuts and two large coffees.

"A dozen?" Suit said. "We're not going to eat a dozen donuts."

"Sooner or later," Jesse said.

Suit put the cruiser in gear.

"Care to dine with an ocean view?" Suit said.

"Sure," Jesse said. "The wharf would do but make it quick. Don't want the donuts to spoil."

"Donuts don't spoil," Suit said and drove them to the wharf.

They left the motor on against the chill as they ate donuts and drank coffee and looked at the boat traffic, even on a cold day, moving about on the harbor.

"Seem like a nice couple," Suit said.

"The Lincolns?"

"Who'd you think I meant," Suit said. "Us?"

"Wise guys don't make sergeant," Jesse said.

Suit grinned.

"You got some problem with the Lincolns?" he said.

"Too nice," Jesse said. "Too cooperative."

"You'd prefer they were surly?"

"Suit, you been studying up," Jesse said. "Surly?"

"I'm a high school grad," Suit said. "I know a bunch of words. Sometimes I say *enticing,* or *symbolic.* What's wrong with the Lincolns?"

"They bother me. Lot of people are a little uncomfortable when the cops come and want to look at your gun."

"They knew nobody got shot with their gun," Suit said.

"Some people would want to check with their attorney before letting us test their weapon," Jesse said. "People are uneasy with cops."

"Maybe, since they had nothing to hide they didn't want to act like they did."

"Maybe," Jesse said.

"Well, soon as we fire the thing we'll know."

"We'll know the bullets that killed our people weren't fired from that gun," Jesse said.

"You think they had another gun?"

"Two."

"You think they did it?"

"Until I got a better suspect," Jesse said, "yes."

"Her too?"

"Yes."

"Even if the gun don't match," Suit said.

"It won't match," Jesse said. "They knew that when they gave it to us."

"You never said nothing to them about their car being parked up at the Paradise Mall when Barbara Carey got killed," Suit said.

He wiped cinnamon sugar off his chin with the back of his hand.

"No need to tell them all we know," Jesse said.

"Because you got some kind of instinct that they're the ones?" Suit said.

"Because there's something very phony about them," Jesse said.

"Lot of that going around in Paradise," Suit said.

"But they're the only phonies whose car was parked ten feet from a homicide," Jesse said.

"Well," Suit said. "Yeah."

44

They sat together on the couch in the living room with their feet up on the coffee table. It was so still that they could hear the small click of the ice maker in their freezer. On the far horizon was the low profile of an oil tanker heading toward Chelsea Creek.

"Looking at the water," he said, "it's like you can see eternity."

With her head resting against his shoulder, she said, "You always say that."

"Well, it's always so."

"It's always so, for you," she said.

"You and I are one and the same," he said.

She was quiet. The oil tanker disappeared behind the coastline curve to the east.

"Do you think the cop will forget about us after the gun doesn't match?" he said.

"He was so polite," she said. "I thought he was nice."

"In an odd way, I hope he doesn't forget about us."

"Makes it more exciting?" she said.

"I guess so," he said.

"What if he catches us?"

"You think he's going to catch us? Him and his bumpkin buddy?"

"He didn't seem to know very much," she said. "Actually I think we sort of intimidated them."

"I know," he said. "Did you see how stiff the big one was sitting by the door?"

The ocean was empty now, stretching out from the empty beach below them. They watched its blue gray movement and the scatter of whitecaps where the wind ruffled the surface.

"They can't find out anything from the gun," she said.

"Of course not," he said. "We haven't even fired the damn thing."

"I know. I just worry sometimes."

"Do you really think some flatfooted cop has a chance against us? You and me?"

"He didn't seem so stupid to me," she said, "more like he was polite."

"He was looking at your ass, for God's sake."

She smiled and banged her head gently against his shoulder.

"See, I told you he wasn't stupid."

He put his hand inside her thigh, and she snuggled down a little against him.

"Do that, myself," he said.

"I know."

Two gulls rose outside their window, effortlessly riding the air currents. They never seemed cold in the winter, nor hot in the summer; they were just always there, circling, soaring, looking for food.

"It might be fun to kill him," he said.

"The cop?"

"Yes."

"Isn't that asking for trouble?"

"Isn't that what we do," he said. "Ask for trouble? Would it be as thrilling doing what we do, if there were no risk of getting caught."

"I suppose you're right," she said. "I never thought of it that way."

"Would you have fun playing baseball if you knew you couldn't lose?" he said.

"I never played baseball," she said.

"Or gambling." He was very intense. "The possibility of losing is what gives it juice."

"It would be something," she said, "afterwards."

"It would," he said, "be the fuck of our lives."

"Oh my," she said.

"We should think about it," he said.

"Yes. Even if we decide to do it, though, we shouldn't do it yet."

"Let's see how close he can get without catching us," he said.

"And then if we kill him," she said, "it will be in the nick of time."

She smiled up at him.

"What kind of fuck would that be?" she said.

45

Together again, Jesse thought, as he looked at Candace Pennington sitting across his conference table from Bo Marino. Chuck Pennington was there with Candace, and Joe Marino was with Bo.

"He threatened Candace," Chuck Pennington said quietly. "He told her if she testified against him he'd kill her, and if he had to he'd kill Feeney too."

"The hell he did," Joe Marino said. "He told her anything it was she should stop lying about him."

"Anyone else hear the threat, Candace?" Jesse said.

"No, but he said it."

"Liar," Bo said.

"See, nobody heard him," Joe Marino said. "It's just his word against hers."

"Don't force me to make that choice," Jesse said.

"What's that mean," Marino said.

"It means that I have found Bo to be a chronic liar, and a bad creep."

"See that, they're all out to get me. I didn't do nothing to the bitch."

Chuck Pennington stood up quite suddenly. He showed no change of expression as he reached across the table and yanked Bo Marino out of his chair and dragged him headfirst over the table.

"Hey," Joe Marino said and stood up.

Chuck Pennington punched Bo twice in the face with his left hand. Bo's father grabbed Chuck from behind and wrestled him away from Bo. Pennington shrugged Marino off, and turned and hit him a right hook that set Marino back on his heels and another one that knocked him down. Jesse put a hand softly on Candace's shoulder. Otherwise he did nothing. Bo floundered across the tabletop, his nose bleeding. He was a big kid, a weight lifter and a football player, but he looked like neither with the blood running down his face and tears welling in his eyes. He swung wildly at Chuck Pennington, who tucked his chin inside his left shoulder and let the punch slide off his arms. Then he hit Bo with a straight left and a right cross and Bo sat down hard on the floor. Bo's father was scrambling to his feet.

"Arrest him," Joe Marino screamed at Jesse. "You saw it. I want the sonovabitch arrested for assault."

"Assault?" Jesse said.

"You seen him," Marino shouted.

"Sit down, Mr. Pennington," Jesse said. "I promise you they won't assault you again."

"Wait a minute," Marino said. "You was sitting right here."

Pennington sat down. He still had no expression on his face but he was breathing a little harder. He didn't look at his daughter, who stared at him with her mouth open.

"And I saw you and your son insult Candace Pennington and assault her father," Jesse said. "You see it any different?"

"That's the way I see it," Chuck Pennington said.

"Me too," Candace said.

Her small voice was startling in the big room.

"He punched my kid for no reason," Marino said.

Bo had gotten to his feet and was holding a paper napkin against his bloody nose. He was crying.

"I think there was a reason, Mr. Marino," Jesse said.

46

Jesse came into the Gray Gull out of the bright winter day, and stood for a minute to let his eyes adjust. The maître d' saw him and came over with some menus under his arm.

"This isn't a raid, is it, Jesse?"

Jesse smiled.

"I'm meeting someone," he said.

"I know, she's here already. I put her by the window, that okay?"

"Swell," Jesse said.

Rita Fiore was sitting sideways to the table with her legs crossed, sipping a glass of white wine. She was wearing a black suit with a long jacket and a short skirt. Her white blouse had a low scoop neck, and the sun reflecting through the window off the harbor made her thick red hair glisten. She smiled at Jesse.

"I feel like I walked into some kind of fashion shoot," Jesse said.

"Yes," Rita said as he sat down. "My plan is that you'll be so taken with my appearance that you'll do whatever I want."

"It's working," Jesse said.

The maître d' put the menu down in front of Jesse, took Jesse's order for a cranberry juice and soda, and departed.

"Thanks for meeting me," Rita said.

"Didn't want to run the press gauntlet?"

"I thought it might be nicer if we stayed away from all of that," Rita said.

She sipped her wine and looked out at the harbor.

"This is a lovely spot," she said. "How's the food?"

"Adequate," Jesse said. "The view's better."

A waiter brought Jesse his cranberry and soda. He looked at Rita's glass, and she shook her head. Sitting across from her, Jesse could feel her energy. There was a sense of intelligence and of kinetic sensuality that radiated from her in equal portions.

"Are you thinking long thoughts?" Rita said.

"Mostly I'm thinking, wow!"

"Good," Rita said. "I like wow."

"In the small moments between thinking wow, I'm wondering why you wanted to see me."

Rita looked at him for a while without speaking. Somehow she managed to sit with a wiggle. *I wonder how she does that?*

"Like so much in life," Rita said, "there are several reasons, including the hope that you might in fact think wow."

Jesse smiled. The waiter came. Rita ordered a Caesar salad. Jesse ordered a club sandwich. The waiter left. Jesse waited.

"First, I now represent only Bo Marino," Rita said.

"Nice," Jesse said.

Rita wrinkled her nose.

"Everyone is entitled to the best defense he can get," she said.

"Which would be you."

"Yes."

"Reagan know?"

"I have so notified the Essex County DA."

"So why tell me?"

Rita smiled.

"Because the Marinos wish to sue you for dereliction of duty."

"Is that in the penal code," Jesse said.

"Not exactly," Rita said. "But pretty much everything is in there if you're a good enough lawyer. They are also suing Chuck Pennington for assault."

"Really?"

"They claim he assaulted them in your presence and you did nothing to prevent it."

"It all happened so quickly," Jesse said.

"I'm sure," Rita said. "I can tell already that you're kind of slow to react."

"Well," Jesse said, "the thing is Bo attacked Chuck, who responded in self-defense. Then Joe Marino jumped in and Chuck had to defend himself from both of them."

"And you?"

"Broke it up as soon as I could," Jesse said. "Restraining the Marinos was difficult."

Rita smiled faintly. "I'm sure," she said.

The club sandwich was cut into four triangles. Jesse picked up one of the triangles and bit off the point.

"And," Rita said. "If I were to talk with the Pennington father and daughter, I'd probably hear the same story."

"Sure," Jesse said.

"Verbatim," Rita said.

Jesse smiled. "We all saw the same thing," Jesse said.

"And that's how you'll all testify."

"Absolutely," Jesse said.

"So it will be your word against theirs."

"And I'm a distinguished law officer here in Paradise," Jesse said. "And Bo is a rapist."

Rita nodded and ate a crouton and looked out at the harbor, and across at Paradise Neck, with Stiles Island at the tip, tethered by the new causeway.

"Did you know that Chuck Pennington was a boxer in college?" she said.

"I did," Jesse said.

Rita ate another crouton and half a romaine leaf.

"Doesn't that make Bo seem kind of foolhardy?" she said.

"Bo isn't smart enough to be foolhardy," Jesse said. "And, of course, he didn't know what Pennington did in college."

"Be hard to demonstrate that he did," Rita said. "Ethically."

"Ethically?"

"I know, it's embarrassing, but . . ." Rita shrugged. "It will be difficult to enlist a jury's sympathy for Bo Marino."

"Who is, you will note," Jesse said, "bigger than Pennington. So is his father."

"Noted," Rita said and finished her wine and waved the empty glass at the waiter.

They ate in silence for the short time it took the waiter to replace Rita's glass.

When he was gone, Rita said, "This isn't a winner for our side. I'll persuade my clients to drop it."

"And if they don't?"

Rita smiled.

"They'll drop it," she said.

Jesse nodded and ate his club sandwich.

"So," Rita said, "off the record, what really happened?"

"Off the record?"

"Between you and me, only," Rita said.

"Pennington smacked the crap out of Bo Marino and his old man, and I let him."

"I'm shocked," Rita said.

"It'll be our secret," Jesse said.

"Perhaps," Rita said, "before we're through there will be several more."

Jesse looked at her and she looked back. There was promise in her eyes, and challenge, and a flash of something so visceral, Jesse thought, that Rita may not have known it was there.

"Wow," Jesse said.

47

Jesse was on the phone with the state police ballistics lab, talking to a technician named Holton. Suitcase Simpson sat across the desk from him, drinking coffee and reading the *Globe*.

"No match," Holton said, "on the murder bullets and the Marlin."

"I didn't expect any," Jesse said.

"Maybe you should wait and send us something that you expect to match," Holton said.

"Got to eliminate it," Jesse said.

"Well, you can eliminate this one," Holton said. "Far as I can tell, it's never been fired."

Jesse was silent, sitting back in his chair, staring out the window.

"You still there?" Holton said.

"Sorry," Jesse said. "I was just thinking."

"You were?" Holton said. "I wasn't sure cops did that in the suburbs."

"Only as a last resort," Jesse said and hung up.

"No match?" Simpson said without looking up from the paper.

"No match," Jesse said.

"Well, it's not like you didn't call it," Simpson said.

"So much for plinking vermin," Jesse said.

"Vermin?" Simpson said

"They said they had the rifle to plink vermin at their summer place."

"So?"

"So according to the state ballistics guy the gun has probably never even been fired."

"Why would they lie about that?" Simpson said.

"To explain why they had the gun."

"Lotta people own a gun they haven't fired."

"Yeah, and they usually have it in the house, for protection."

"So why wouldn't they just say that?"

"Because they are too smart for their own good," Jesse said. "They think we would wonder why they'd buy a twenty-two rifle for protection."

"A twenty-two will kill you," Simpson said.

"As well we know," Jesse said.

"So if they said it was for protection, would we wonder?"

"Maybe," Jesse said, "we're supposed to wonder."

"Maybe they were just embarrassed at keeping a gun for protection, and said it was for vermin," Simpson said.

"They look embarrassed to you?" Jesse said.

"No. You think they got two other guns?"

"Handguns," Jesse said. "You wouldn't use a rifle for the kind of killing they did."

"If they did it," Simpson said.

"I think they did," Jesse said.

"You always tell me, Jesse, don't be in a hurry to decide stuff."

"I want to know everything about Tony and Brianna," Jesse said. "Phone records, credit cards, dates of birth, social security numbers, previous residences, when they were married, where they lived before this, where the country home is where they are not plinking vermin, do they have relatives, who are their friends, what do the neighbors know about them, where he practiced medicine, where they went to school."

"You want me to pick the gun up first and return it? Or you want me to start digging into the Lincolns."

"I'll take care of the rifle," Jesse said. "You start digging."

Simpson nodded.

"Can I finish reading *Arlo and Janis*?" Simpson said.

"No."

48

The resident cars at Seascape were parked behind the building at the end of a winding drive, in a blacktop parking lot with a card-activated one-armed gate at the entrance. Jesse was driving his own car, and he parked it across from Seascape on a side street perpendicular to the point where the drive wound into Atlantic Avenue. He had far too many things under way, he knew, to be doing hopeful surveillance. But Jesse was the only cop on the force who was good at it. Any of the Paradise cops could do an open tail, Jesse knew. But he didn't want the Lincolns to know they were being tailed, and getting spooky on him. He was the only one he trusted to do an undiscovered tail. He couldn't cover them all the time. During the day he was too busy, but the nights were quieter, *and half a tail is better than none,* he thought, so each night after work he drove over here and parked and waited.

He knew it was them. He couldn't prove it, not even enough to get a search warrant, but he'd been a cop nearly half his life, and he knew. He had the advantage on them for the moment. They didn't know that he knew. They thought he was just the local bumpkin chief of a small department, and they felt superior to him. He knew that as surely as he knew they were guilty. And that too gave him an advantage. He'd watched their body language and listened to them talk and heard the undertones in their voices. He was nothing. He couldn't possibly catch them. Jesse had no intention of changing their minds.

"I love arrogance," Jesse said aloud in the dark interior of his silent car.

At ten minutes past seven he saw the red Saab pull out of the drive and head east on Atlantic Avenue. He slid into gear and pulled out a considerable distance behind them. After a while he pulled up closer, and where Atlantic had a long stretch with only one cross street, which was one way into the avenue, he turned off and went around the block and rejoined Atlantic just after they passed.

Jesse had already shadowed them three nights that week. Once they had eaten pizza, at a place in the village. Once they had food shopped at the Paradise Mall. Once they had gone to a movie. Each time it got more boring, and each time Jesse tailed them as if it would lead to their arrest.

He let himself drop two cars back of the Saab as they went through the village and over the hill toward downtown. The other cars peeled off and when they turned east near the town wharf, Jesse was directly behind them. They drove for a little while with the harbor on their right, until the Saab pulled into the parking lot at Jesse's apartment.

Jesse drove on by and parked around the bend. He walked down behind the condominiums, and stood at the corner of the building next to his, in the shadows, and watched. The Saab was quiet. The lights were out. The motor had been turned off. The parking lot was lit with mercury lamps, which deepened the shadow in which Jesse stood. The moon was bright. The passenger-side window of the Saab slid down. In the passenger seat, Brianna held something up and pointed an object at Jesse's apartment. On the other side of his condo the harbor waters moving made a pleasant sound. The object was a camera and Jesse realized that she was taking pictures of his home.

After ten minutes the window rolled back up. The Saab remained. Nothing moved. Nothing happened. After half an hour the Saab engine turned over. The lights went on. And the Saab pulled out of the lot. Jesse made no attempt to follow. Instead he drove back to Seascape, taking his time, and checked the parking lot. The Saab was there. Jesse looked at the clock on his dashboard. 9:40. All of him was tired. His legs felt heavy. His shoulders were hunched. His eyes kept closing on him.

"You can only do what you can do," Jesse said aloud, and turned the car and went home.

49

Jesse was in the Essex County Court in Salem, sitting in a conference room with Martin Reagan, the ADA on the case, Rita Fiore, and lawyers for Feeney and Drake. Feeney's lawyer was a husky dark-eyed woman named Emily Frank, and Drake was represented by a loud-voiced man with a full white beard named Richard DeLuca.

"We don't have to consult you, Jesse," Reagan said. "But we thought your input might be useful in arriving at a plea bargain."

Jesse nodded. Rita smiled at him. Jesse could feel the smile in his stomach.

"None of these boys is a hardened criminal," Rita said. "All of them are under eighteen. We're thinking of no jail time."

"They need jail time," Jesse said.

"We were thinking probation, counseling, and community service," Rita said.

Jesse shook his head.

"They need jail time," he said. "Doesn't have to be long, and it doesn't have to be hard time. It can be in a juvenile facility. But they gang-raped a sixteen-year-old-girl and photographed her naked and threatened her and harassed her."

"Hell, Chief, weren't you ever a teenage boy? They're hormones with feet."

"I was," Jesse said. "And my hormones were jumping through my skin like everybody else's. But I never raped anyone, did you?"

"We're not condoning what they did," Emily Frank said. "Richard was just suggesting that their youth made them less able to control themselves."

"You think they didn't know it was wrong?" Jesse said.

The lawyers were quiet.

"You think they couldn't control themselves?"

"Well," Rita said. "They didn't."

"No they didn't," Jesse said.

Rita met his eyes, and again he could feel it.

"But what purpose is served by locking these children up?" Emily Frank said.

"You know that scale of justice, outside. What they did

to Candace Pennington will tip it pretty far down, and it will take a lot more than probation and community service to balance it out."

"Well," Reagan said. "What would you recommend."

"I recommend that I take each one into a spare cell and beat the crap out of him and send him home."

"You can't do that," Emily Frank said.

"I know," Jesse said. "It's too simple."

"It's barbaric," Emily Frank said.

Rita looked mildly amused.

"And illegal," Emily Frank said.

"I know."

"What would they learn about right and wrong from that?"

"Nothing," Jesse said. "But they'd know what hurts and what doesn't."

"Thanks for your input, Jesse," Reagan said. "We'll go it alone from here."

Jesse nodded and stood up. He felt Rita watching him.

"I think you should know," Emily Frank said, "that I for one haven't found this meeting useful."

"I never thought it would be," Jesse said, and walked out of the room.

Rita followed him.

"This will take all day," she said "Are you free for dinner?"

"Sure," Jesse said.

"I'll pick something up and come to your place."

"Really," Jesse said.

"About seven," Rita said.

"Seven," Jesse said.

Rita turned and walked back along the second-floor corridor to the conference room. At the door she turned.

"Probably eat about nine or ten," she said and grinned and went in.

50

The town beach was empty, except for a woman in a pink down jacket running a Jack Russell terrier. Jesse stood for a moment under the little pavilion that served, as far as Jesse could tell, no useful purpose. Twenty feet to his left Kenneth Eisley's body had rolled about at the tidal margin, until the ocean receded. The first one. Jesse looked out at the rim of the gray ocean, where it merged with the gray sky. It seemed longer ago than it was. They'd found him in November, and now it was the start of February. Dog was still with Valenti. Too long. Dog shouldn't be in a shelter that long. *I got to find someone to take the dog.* Beaches were cold places in February. Jesse was wearing a turtleneck and a sheepskin jacket. He pulled his watch cap down over his ears, and pushed his hands into the pockets of his coat. *I know who killed you, Kenneth.* He stepped off the little pavilion and onto the sand. He was above the high tide line where the mingle of seaweed and flotsam made a ragged line. Ahead of him the Jack Russell raced down at the ocean as it rolled in and barked at it, and dodged back when it got close. He was taunting the ocean. *I know who killed the lady in the mall, and the guy in the church parking lot. I know who killed Abby.* Jesse trudged along the sand, feeling it shift slightly beneath his feet as he walked. *Now me?* He could think of no reasonable explanation for why they would go out in the evening and take pictures of his home. The day was not windy, and the ocean's movement was gently rounded, with only an occasional crest of the waves. There was something about oceans. The day he left LA he went to Santa Monica and looked at the Pacific. Despite their perpetual movement there was a stillness about oceans. Despite the sound of the waves, there was a great silence. The empty beach and the limitless ocean hinted at the vast secret of things. He'd gotten their attention. They were reacting to him. It was a start. *If I stay with them maybe they'll make a run at me, and I'll have them.* He smiled to himself. *Or they'll have me.* He stopped and looked out at the ocean. High up, a single herring gull circled slowly above the ocean, looking down, hoping for food. Nothing moved on the horizon. *I guess if they get me I won't care much.* In front of him the Jack Russell yapped urgently at his owner. She took a ball from her backpack and threw it awkwardly, the way girls throw. The dog raced after it. Caught up with it, pounced on it with his forepaws, bumped it with his nose, grabbed it in his mouth and shook it to death.

Looking at the ocean, Jesse thought about Abby. She hadn't found the man of her dreams. She'd hoped that Jesse would make her happy, but he hadn't. Nothing much did. She wanted things too hard, she needed things too much, she had her own private fight with alcohol. Sometimes her sexuality embarrassed her. The gull had moved inland, looking for landfill or roadkill, or maybe a discarded Moon Pie. Nothing moved above the ocean now. *I wish I could have loved you, Abby.* He reached the end of the beach, where the huge sea-smooth rocks loomed up, and beyond them, expensive houses with a view. *So long, Ab.* He turned and started back along the beach. The Jack Russell had left too, joining his owner in a silver Audi coupe, just pulling out of the parking lot. The dog had his head out the window, and though it was far away, Jesse could faintly hear him yapping. The cold air was clean off the ocean, and he liked the way it felt as it went into his lungs. *I wonder if they are going to try to kill me.* When he got to the aimless little pavilion Jesse paused again and looked out at the ocean again. Nothing alive was in sight. He was alone. He breathed in, and stood listening to the quiet sound of the ocean, and the soft sound of his breathing. *I wonder if they will succeed.*

51

Jenn was always late. Most of the women Jesse knew were late. Rita was there at seven. She carried her purse over her shoulder, a small bag that might have been a briefcase over the other shoulder, and in her arms a large paper bag. She handed him the bag when he opened the door.

"I am beautiful and dangerous," Rita said. "But I don't carry things very well."

Jesse took the bag and backed away from the door.

"I'm glad to see you," he said.

"And I you," she said. "The plea bargaining was interminable."

"Four lawyers in a room," Jesse said.

Rita put her purse and her shoulder bag on the living room floor next to the coffee table.

"No wonder they hate lawyers," Rita said. "For crissake, I hate lawyers . . . except me."

Jesse smiled. He took the paper bag to the kitchen and set it on the counter.

"Shall I unload?" he said.

"Sure. I like domesticity in a man," Rita said.

Jesse took out a bottle of Riesling, two kinds of cheese, a big sausage, two loaves of French bread, some red grapes, some green grapes, and four green apples.

"Would you like some of this wine?" Jesse said.

"I brought it in case," Rita said. "What I'd actually like, if you have it, is a very large, very dry martini."

"Sure," Jesse said. "Gin or vodka?"

"You have Ketel One?"

"I do."

"Yes," she said.

Jesse made the martini in a silver shaker, plopped two big olives in a wide martini glass, and poured Rita a drink.

"Aren't you having something?" she said.

Jesse shook his head.

"I don't drink," he said.

"Didn't you used to," Rita said.

"I did," Jesse said. "Now I don't."

He was a little startled at the firmness with which he said it.

"Get something," Rita said, "a glass of water, anything. I hate to drink alone."

Jesse went to the refrigerator and poured himself a glass of orange juice. He brought it into the living room and sat opposite Rita, who was on the sofa.

"That a boy," Rita said. "Get your vitamins."

Jesse grinned. "How'd the plea bargaining come out," he said.

"Nothing you'd like. They get three years' probation, mandatory counseling, and a hundred and twenty hours each of community service."

"And Candace gets her life ruined," Jesse said.

"I'm a lawyer," Rita said. "I represent my client."

"I know," Jesse said.

Rita put her feet up on Jesse's coffee table. She was wearing a tailored beige suit with a fitted jacket and a short skirt. Jesse admired her legs.

"And," Rita said, "people recover from rape."

"I guess so," Jesse said. "And maybe she will. But she doesn't think so now."

Rita stared at him.

"My God," she said. "You really care about her."

"Right now," Jesse said, "home alone, maybe in her room listening to CDs, she cannot imagine going to school tomorrow. She cannot imagine facing all the kids who will know that she was gang-raped and photographed naked. And the three guys who did it will be in the same high school, maybe the same class, certainly the same cafeteria. . . . Think back, when you were sixteen."

Rita crossed her ankles on the coffee table. She was wearing dark high heels with pointed toes and thin ankle straps.

She sipped her martini and stared at her shoes for a moment while she swallowed slowly.

"I represented Marino. My job, since I couldn't get him off, was to bargain for the best deal he could get. The other lawyers jumped in with me, and we came up with a package deal. I did a good job. While I am," Rita smiled at him, "no longer a little girl, I am a woman, and as a woman I sympathize with the girl. But I wasn't hired to be a woman."

"A lot of the kids in her school will think she was probably asking for it, and they'll think she finked to the cops, and ruined it for three good guys including their football star."

Rita took another sip of martini.

"I know," she said.

They were silent. Rita looked past her martini glass at something very distant. Jesse drank some orange juice.

"I saw the pictures, of course," Rita said. "Spread-eagled naked on the ground. Raped, photographed . . . to them she was just another form of masturbation."

Jesse was silent.

"A sex toy," Rita said. "A thing."

They were both quiet. Rita finished her martini. Jesse poured the rest of the shaker into her glass. She took two olives from the small bowl on the coffee table and plomped them into her drink.

"The court going to specify the community service?" Jesse said.

"They'll leave it to the prosecution. Once they're sentenced we'll get together with Reagan and decide something. Usually the prosecution consults the schools."

"You have any input in this?"

"Informally, sure. Besides, Reagan wants to score me."

"Don't blame him," Jesse said. "Who supervises their service?"

"The court, in theory. In fact the people they're assigned to serve with are supposed to keep track of their hours, and rat them out if they don't do what they're supposed to."

"Which often makes community service a joke," Jesse said.

"Often," Rita said.

"How about they serve their sentence with me?" Jesse said.

Rita stared at him and began to smile.

"They sweep up," Jesse said, "empty trash, run errands, shovel snow, keep the cruisers clean . . . like that."

Rita smiled at him some more.

"And you would, of course, take your supervisory responsibilities seriously," she said.

"I would bust their chops," Jesse said.

"I'll see what I can do," Rita said.

She put her martini glass down and stood and stepped around the coffee table and straddled him where he sat on the leather hassock and sat on his lap facing him. The movement lifted her short skirt almost to her waist. She pressed her mouth against his. After a time she leaned back.

"If I could use your shower," she said, "I'd fluff up my body a little."

"Down the hall on the right, off my bedroom."

Jesse's voice sounded hoarse to him.

"Conveniently located," Rita said.

She stood, smoothed her short skirt over her thighs, and walked to the bathroom.

52

It had begun to snow softly when Jesse pulled into the
visitor's parking space near the Seascape entrance. The same
elegant and careful concierge tried not to stare at the rifle he
was carrying as she phoned the Lincolns.

"Penthouse floor," she said.

"I remember," Jesse said.

Lincoln was waiting for him again, in the small foyer.

"Oh," he said, "my gun."

Jesse handed it to him. Lincoln smiled.

"It's not linked to any drive-by shootings or anything?"
Lincoln said.

"None that we could discover," Jesse said. "And it wasn't
used to kill the four people in Paradise."

"Oh good."

Brianna Lincoln came into the living room.

"Mr. Stone," she said. "What a nice surprise."

"Jesse was just returning our rifle, Brianna."

Lincoln smiled again.

"He said it has not been involved in any crime."

"I'll put it away," Brianna said. "Can I get you coffee, Mr. Stone?"

"Jesse. Sure, that would be fine."

"Cream, two sugars?"

"Yes, ma'am."

She smiled.

"Brianna," she said. "Ma'am is my mother."

Jesse sat, as he had before, looking through the picture window at the ocean. The snow continued softly, blurring the view.

Lincoln laughed.

"I feel like I ought to apologize," he said. "If it had been my gun, it would have made things so much easier for you."

Jesse smiled.

"Think how I feel," Jesse said.

Brianna came back with Jesse's coffee in a stainless steel mug. She put a doily down on the end table near him and set the coffee cup on it.

"Thank you."

She smiled at him warmly. He smiled back.

"You have respect for your tools," Jesse said. "The gun was clean."

"Any tool works best if it's well maintained."

Jesse glanced around the living room.

"This is a great room," he said.

"Yes," Brianna said. "We love it."

Jesse stood and walked to the window.

"On a cop's salary," Jesse said, "I'll never get a view like this."

Both Tony and Brianna smiled modestly.

"We were lucky, I guess," Brianna said. "And Tony is brilliant."

"I can see that," Jesse said.

He turned slowly, looking around the room.

"How big is this place?" he said.

"We have the whole top floor," Lincoln said.

Brianna smiled.

"Would you like a tour?" she said.

"I sure would," Jesse said.

"Come on then," she said.

Tony went with them as she took Jesse through the den with its huge electronic entertainment center, into the luminous kitchen, through the formal dining room, past three large baths, and into the vast bedroom with its canopy bed and another entertainment center. The bed was covered with a thick white silk comforter.

"The workbench," Tony said, nodding at the bed.

"Wow," Jesse said. "You must not have any kids or dogs living here."

"Brianna and I decided against children," Tony said. "We

met in our late thirties, by which time our lives were simply too full for children."

Jesse nodded, looking at the big room, taking it in.

"Any family at all?" Jesse said absently.

"No," Tony said. "We are all the family each other has."

Jesse nodded, obviously dazzled by their wealth and taste, as they walked back to the living room. He sat and picked up his coffee and sipped it.

"Where'd you two meet?" he said, making conversation.

"He picked me up in a bar," Brianna said. "In Cleveland of all places."

"It was an upscale bar," Tony said with a smile.

"I'll bet it was," Jesse said. "Are you both from Cleveland?"

"I am," Brianna said. "Shaker Heights. Tony was doing his residency at Case Western."

"What did you do?" Jesse said.

"I was a lawyer."

"How long have you been married?"

"Fifteen years. I don't think we've ever had an argument."

"That's great," Jesse said.

"Do you have any leads in this serial thing, other than the fact that the victims were shot with a twenty-two?" Tony said.

"Nothing much," Jesse said.

He made a rueful little smile.

"That's why I was pinning my hopes on you," he said.

They all laughed.

"Oh well," Brianna said.

They laughed again.

"Would you like more coffee?" Tony said.

"No, I really should be going," Jesse said.

"If it had been us," Tony said, "why on earth would we want to do such a thing?"

"Everybody needs a hobby," Jesse said.

They laughed.

"Seriously though," Tony said. "Why would we do something like that?"

"Both of you?" Jesse said.

Tony shrugged and nodded.

"A shared sickness, I'd guess," Jesse said.

Tony laughed.

"At least we'd be sharing," he said.

53

"They were flirting with me," Jesse said.

Dix sat silently back in his chair, one foot on the edge of a desk drawer, resting his chin on his steepled hands. His fingernails gleamed quietly. *He always looks like he's just scrubbed for surgery,* Jesse thought.

"Especially the husband," Jesse said.

"Tell me about the flirting," Dix said.

"He kept coming back to the killings. I was trying, sort of indirectly, to learn a little about them. Whenever I'd ask a question, you know, like, where'd you two meet? he'd steer us back to the killings."

Dix nodded.

"And you're convinced it's them," Dix said.

"I've been a cop nearly all my adult life," Jesse said. "It's them."

"We often know things," Dix said. "Before we can demonstrate them."

"I need to demonstrate it," Jesse said.

Dix smiled

"Ain't that a bitch," he said.

"How come," Jesse said, "that sometimes you talk like one of the guys on the corner, and sometimes you sound like Sigmund Freud?"

"Depends what I'm talking about," Dix said.

"Talk about the Lincolns," Jesse said.

Dix nodded without saying anything, as if to confirm that he'd expected Jesse to ask. He took in a lot of air and let it out slowly.

"One of the reasons that psychiatry doesn't have a better reputation is that it is asked to do too many things it doesn't do well," he said.

"Like explaining people you've never met?"

"Like that," Dix said. "Or predicting what they're going to do."

"Not good at that either?"

Dix smiled.

"No worse than anyone else," he said.

"Well, tell me what you can," Jesse said. "I won't hold you to it."

Dix leaned back in his chair.

"Well," he said. "People do not repetitively and freely do things that they don't like to do."

"Why would they like this?"

"We may never know. They may not know."

"Speculate," Jesse said.

"Well, certainly it could give one a feeling of power, and the more one did it, and the more one got away with it, the more power one would feel."

"Hell," Jesse said. "I know it doesn't prove they were powerful. But he was a doctor, and a successful inventor. She was a lawyer. They appear rich."

"Power is in the perception," Dix said.

"You're saying maybe they didn't feel powerful."

"Maybe not," Dix said. "Or maybe they didn't have a shared power."

"His power, her power, not their power?"

Dix shrugged.

"Or," he said, "perhaps it is a bonding ritual."

"Explain," Jesse said.

"They're a couple, and this makes their coupleness special."

"The family that kills together, stays together?"

"They have a shared secret. They have a shared special-ness. Ordinary couples are leading ordinary lives: food shopping, changing diapers, having sex maybe once or twice a month, because they're supposed to. These people have found a thing to share that no one else has."

"Serial killing?"

"Each has the other's guilty secret," Dix said. "It binds them together."

"For crissake, they do this for love?"

"They do this for emotional reasons," Dix said.

"And love is an emotion."

"Love, or what they may think is love," Dix said.

"What might they think is love?"

"Mutual need, mutual mistrust, that needs to be overcome by mutual participation in something that ties them together."

Jesse thought about this. Dix waited.

"Will they keep doing this?" Jesse said.

"No reason for them to stop."

"Why was he flirting with me about this?" Jesse said.

"Maybe the same reason people like to have sex in nearly public places," Dix said.

"Phone booths and movie theaters," Jesse said. "Stuff like that?"

"The danger of being caught increases the guilty pleasure."

"So they know it's wrong?"

"The Lincolns? Sure. Its wrongness is its appeal."

"What will they do next?"

"I have no idea," Dix said. "What I've been giving you are informed, or at least experienced, guesses. I've talked with a lot of wackos in my life. All I can say by way of answer is that there is often an element of ritual in these kinds of crimes, and thus they would tend to keep repeating the ritual."

"Doing the same thing over and over."

"Yes."

"In exactly the same way?" Jesse said.

"Yes."

"Why do you suppose they were photographing my home?"

"I don't know," Dix said. "Maybe they like to first possess the victim's image."

"Victim?"

"What do you think?"

"I think they want to kill me next."

"They might," Dix said.

54

It was snowing again. Pleasantly. Not the hard nasty snowfall of a Northeast storm. This was the kind of fluffy downfall that would leave the town looking like a winter wonderland. In a day or two, the reemerging sun, and the strewn salt from the streets, would shrink it in upon itself, and it would become an implacable mix of dirt and ice, marked by dogs, and littered by people. But right now it was pretty.

"Pretty doesn't have a long shelf life," Jesse said.

"Are you speaking of the snow?" Marcy said. "Or me."

They were on the sofa looking through the window in the living room of her small house in the old downtown section of Paradise where the winding streets made the pre-revolutionary town seem older than it was. Marcy was drinking white wine. Jesse had club soda and cranberry juice.

"Snow," Jesse said. "It'll be ugly by Thursday."

"And I won't."

"No," Jesse said. "You got a long time yet."

Marcy was wearing a gray dress. She had kicked off her heels and put her stocking feet beside Jesse's on the coffee table. Jesse drank some cranberry and soda.

"No wonder you have a drinking problem," Marcy said. "You drink a lot of whatever's in front of you."

"Yeah, but think how clean my urinary tract is," Jesse said.

"Well, that's certainly a comfort," Marcy said.

They were quiet, watching the snow. There was a small fireplace faced with maroon tiles on the far wall of Marcy's living room. Jesse had made a fire.

"How long since you've had a drink," Marcy said.

"Two weeks."

"Good for you," Marcy said.

"I don't drink anymore," Jesse said.

"You're so sure?"

"Yes."

"Whatever happened to 'one day at a time'?"

"I know what I know," Jesse said.

"You think you'll ever drink again?"

"Not to excess," Jesse said.

"You're so sure."

"I am."

"What happened?"

"I don't know," Jesse said. "Stuff changes."

"How about Jenn," Marcy said. "How is she?"

"Don't know. I haven't seen her in a couple of weeks, either."

"Will you see her again?"

"Yes," Jesse said.

"So some stuff doesn't change."

"Maybe it does," Jesse said. "Just not as, what? . . . not as simply as yes or no."

"Relationships are hard," Marcy said.

"Except ours," Jesse said.

"We have a great advantage in ours," Marcy said. "We don't love each other."

"I know," Jesse said.

They each took a drink. The snow came down very smoothly past the window.

"You got the kids that raped that girl," Marcy said.

"Yes. They copped to a plea. Probation and community service."

"No jail?"

"No jail," Jesse said. "Kids. First offense . . ."

Jesse smiled slightly.

"On the other hand," he said, "their community service assignment is me."

"You rigged that, didn't you."

"I did."

"Well, maybe they will get a taste of justice, at least."

"Candace won't," Jesse said.

"You think she won't get over it?"

"I think the other kids won't let her."

"Some of them will be kind," Marcy said.

"And some of them won't," Jesse said.

"And you can't protect her."

"No," Jesse said. "I can't."

"Well," Marcy said. "You did what you could, you closed the case."

"You been hanging around with me too long," Jesse said. "You're starting to talk like a cop."

"Or at least like you," Marcy said.

"I'm a cop," Jesse said.

"I know."

"Sometimes I think that's all I am, everything I am."

"There are worse things," Marcy said.

Jesse smiled at her.

"Like serial killing?" Jesse said.

"That would be worse," Marcy said. "Are you getting anywhere with that?"

"Yes and no," Jesse said. "I know who they are. I can't prove it."

"Who are they?"

"A couple, live over in the Seascape condos."

"By Preston Beach," she said.

"Yep."

"What are their names."

"Tony and Brianna Lincoln," Jesse said.

"My God," Marcy said. "I think I showed them a house once."

"Recently?"

"No, maybe three years ago. Before they bought their condo."

"Form any impressions?"

"No, yes, actually, I did. They were a pleasure. You know, you bring a husband and wife to look at property and they usually are on each other's case the whole trip. The Lincolns were great, really together. I remember thinking how nice it is to see that. He's not scornful of her questions about the house. She doesn't smirk at me when he speaks. They acted like people who liked each other and respected each other's ideas."

Jesse laughed a little.

"Still do," he said.

"And you know it's them?"

"There's some evidence. They own twenty-two ammunition. Their car was parked in the row next to the one where the woman was killed at the Paradise Mall. A car that resembled their car, we didn't get a number, was parked in the church lot where the guy got killed coming home from the train. But we have no hard evidence. No ballistics, no prints, no eyewitness—God knows, no motive."

"And you can't just arrest them on cop-ly intuition?"

"Doesn't seem fair, does it," Jesse said

"So what will you do?"

"We're excavating their past," Jesse said, "which seems to have taken place in Cleveland. We're trying to keep an eye on them twenty-four/seven."

"You sound like that's hard."

"It is, in a small department in a small town. My guys haven't much experience."

"You do."

"Yes, I do," Jesse said. "But I can't spend all day and night keeping them under surveillance. I have to eat, to sleep, to conduct other police business, to fuck you."

"Yes, fucking me is important."

"Right now it seems like the only thing I'm any good at," Jesse said.

"Pays to specialize," Marcy said. "And if you're fishing for a compliment, you are very good."

"Thank you."

"State police can't help with the surveillance?" Marcy said.

"They've taken over the routine night patrols for us," Jesse said.

"How about the gun, they must have a gun, if they buy bullets."

"We test-fired it," Jesse said. "The gun they own didn't fire the bullets that killed the victims."

"So all you can do is watch and wait?"

"Maybe something will turn up in Cleveland."

"And if it doesn't?"

"We do have one other small something."

"Really?"

"They came out one night after supper and took pictures of my home."

"You saw them?"

"I tailed them there," Jesse said.

"Well, what on earth . . ."

"Don't know," Jesse said. "But they seem to have an interest in me and maybe we can encourage them to develop it."

"Interest?" Marcy said "What kind of interest."

"Don't know yet, but we know that they have one."

"Both of them, you think?"

"Two guns," Jesse said.

"So these people have an interest in killing people, and now they seem interested in you?"

"Is it a great country," Jesse said, "or what."

Marcy took a sip of wine and stared at him for a time without swallowing. She took a deep breath in through her nose, and, finally, swallowed her wine.

"You are going to be bait," she said.

"Careful bait," Jesse said.

"My God, how can you be careful bait?"

"Body armor, stay alert," Jesse said.

"Maybe we're not in love," Marcy said. "But you are the dearest friend I've ever had. I would be devastated if you got killed too."

"Good to know someone would," Jesse said. "But I'm pretty good at this."

"Better than they are?"

"Maybe we'll find out," Jesse said.

"If I could talk you out of it, I would," Marcy said. "But I can't."

Jesse nodded. Marcy emptied her wineglass. Jesse took the bottle from the ice bucket and poured her half a glass more.

"So," she said, "my fallback position is *let's fuck*."

Jesse grinned at her. Her dress had buttons all the way down the front.

"It's important to keep my hand in," he said.

Marcy began to unbutton the dress.

"Or whatever," she said.

55

Suitcase Simpson came into Jesse's office with a thick manila folder.

"I heard back from Cleveland," he said.

Jesse gestured to a chair. Simpson sat down and put the folder in his lap and opened it.

Simpson said, "Anthony Lincoln was in fact a resident in ophthalmology at Case Western Medical Center from 1985 to 1990. He married Brianna Douglass in 1988. Her address at that time was twelve twenty-one Buckeye Road, which is in Shaker Heights. Her occupation was listed as attorney."

"Either of them have a record?"

"No."

"Cleveland cops have unsolved serial-type killings?"

"One case, not really a clear-cut serial thing. In 1989, a cabbie was shot in his car on Euclid Ave., presumably by a passenger, two in the back of the head. In 1990 a seventeen-year-old girl was shot at a bus stop in Parma, which is near Cleveland."

"I know where Parma is," Jesse said.

"Two in the chest."

Jesse nodded.

"Both people were killed with twenty-twos."

"Same gun?" Jesse said.

"No. Cabbie and the girl were both killed with the same two guns, one shot each time from each gun."

"Hello," Jesse said.

"Then it stopped. Cleveland can't find any connection between the cabbie and the girl. Neighborhoods are different. They never found the gun. No clues. Nothing."

"You got someone you're talking to at Case Western?"

"Yeah, broad in the administration office."

"Call her back, find out where Tony Lincoln's first post-residency position was, and when he took it."

"Roger."

"And while you're at it," Jesse said, "see if you can find out where Tony did his undergraduate work."

"Why?"

"Why not?" Jesse said.

"Jeez," Simpson said. "No wonder you're the chief and I'm just a patrolman."

"And get hold of the Ohio Bar Association," Jesse said. "Find out whatever you can about Brianna Douglass Lincoln."

Simpson wrote himself a note in a little yellow spiral-bound notepad that he took from his shirt pocket.

"When I go out," he said, "and the press asks me what's up, does this permit me to say we're following up several leads?"

"It does," Jesse said. "Call them promising leads if you want."

"Yeah," Simpson said. "Promising leads. I like it."

After Simpson left, Jesse sat and looked out the window. The TV trucks were still parked across the street. Anthony deAngelo and Eddie Cox were wasting important man-hours keeping the press at bay, and the traffic moving past the trucks. A young man with longish hair, a microphone, and a trench coat was standing in the snow on the lawn, do-ing a stand-up in front of the station. It seemed to Jesse that all day someone was doing a stand-up. He wondered how many people in the viewing audience were tired of seeing the front door of the Paradise Police Station.

Across the street a red Saab sedan pulled up and stopped in a space between two television trucks, with the passen-ger side facing the station house. The window slid silently down. Jesse got a pair of binoculars from a file drawer and focused in on the car. Brianna Lincoln was holding a cam-era, filming the scene. After several minutes, she put the camera down. The window slid silently up. And the Saab pulled away.

Nothing really incriminating. Half a dozen people had come by since the circus had started, and taken pictures. Jesse rocked slowly against the spring in his swivel chair. *Nobody had gone to his house and photographed him, though. Just the Lincolns. Formerly of Cleveland. Why had they taken pictures of where he lived?*

The closet in Jesse's office was located so that one had to close the office door to open the closet. Jesse did so, and opened the closet door and took out a Kevlar vest. He hefted it, not so heavy. He slipped it on and fastened the Velcro. He put his jacket on over it and zipped up the front. It looked okay. It should work okay, too. Unless they changed their MO.

56

The three boys stood uneasily in front of Jesse's desk.

"Miss Fiore said we was supposed to come here after school," Bo said.

None of the three was defiant. None of them met Jesse's gaze.

"You understand why you're here," Jesse said.

"Community service," Bo said.

"Which the court requires of you."

They nodded.

"Why?" Jesse said.

"'Cause of Candace," Kevin Feeney said.

"What about Candace?" Jesse said.

"Oh come on, man, you know."

"Don't call me 'man,'" Jesse said. "All three of you copped to raping her. Is that right?"

Bo said, "Yes, sir."

The other two nodded.

"So you are not some public-spirited high school kids, doing some volunteer chores," Jesse said. "You are three convicted rapists."

They all nodded.

"Just so we're clear," Jesse said.

They all nodded again.

"I regret that you're not doing time," Jesse said. "And if you fuck up here, maybe I can still get you some. You understand?"

Bo Marino said, "Yes, sir."

The other two nodded.

"I have no respect for you," Jesse said.

The three boys didn't say anything. They didn't look at Jesse or each other.

"I think you three are punks."

None of the three had any answer.

"I am going to make your time here as unpleasant as possible," Jesse said.

The three boys looked at the floor. Jesse looked at them for a while without speaking.

"Okay," he said finally, "go see Officer Crane at the front desk. She'll tell you what to do."

57

Jesse sat drinking coffee with Captain Healy in the front seat of his Ford Explorer, while the fine snow came down steadily in the parking lot behind the courthouse in downtown Salem.

"You have everything you need but evidence," Healy said.

"That's all that's missing," Jesse said.

"Except motive."

"Well, yeah, that too."

"Gee," Healy said. "Hot on the trail."

"They did it," Jesse said.

"I believe you," Healy said. "But I'm not the one that needs to believe you."

"I know," Jesse said.

He drank some coffee.

"I can't even get a search warrant."

"Judges hate to issue them on cop intuition," Healy said. "Want some surveillance help?"

"No," Jesse said.

"Might prevent them from killing the next one," Healy said.

"I think I'm the next one," Jesse said.

Healy looked at him and raised his eyebrows and didn't say anything.

"They've been taking pictures," Jesse said.

"Of what?"

"My home, the station."

Healy frowned, watching the steam rise from the triangular tear in the plastic top of his coffee cup.

"They're interested in you," Healy said.

"I'd say so."

"And they're serial killers," Healy said.

"I'm convinced of it."

"And they kill people at random, for no obvious reason," Healy said.

"They seem to."

The snowflakes were very small, and with no wind they fell straight down, like white rain.

"You figure you're being penciled in as their next victim," Healy said.

"Yes."

"And you figure the picture-taking is foreplay?"

"Something like that."

Healy said, "I can give you a couple of troopers to watch your back."

Jesse shook his head.

"This might be an opportunity," Jesse said.

"They try to kill you and you catch them in the act?"

"Yeah."

"Serial killers like ritual," Healy said. "So they'll come at you from the front, and shoot you one time each."

"Probably at the same time."

"Simultaneous climax," Healy said. "You think you can keep them from killing you?"

"Yes."

"You trust them to come at you the same way," Healy said.

"People like these people, they'll do it the same."

"Let's hope so," Healy said.

"And, if I fuck up," Jesse said, "you can avenge me."

58

It was twenty minutes to midnight when Jenn called and woke Jesse up.

"I just did the eleven-o'clock news," Jenn said. "Did I wake you."

"No," Jesse said. "I was awake."

"Your voice sounds like you were sleeping," Jenn said.

"I'm awake," Jesse said.

"I wanted to apologize," Jenn said.

"Okay."

"You *were* sleeping."

"And you called to apologize for waking me?"

"No, silly, for the other day, when I wanted you to give me special access."

"Which is more than I get," Jesse said.

"I know," Jenn said. "But what was so bad about it was, here you are with this huge serial killer problem to deal with, and I'm thinking only about what would be best for me."

"What's new," Jesse said.

Jenn was silent for a moment.

"Well," she said. "You *are* grouchy."

"I am," Jesse said.

"It's okay," Jenn said. "You deserve to be."

"Thanks."

"What I want you to know is that I realize I was thinking only about myself and my career when I asked you to let me in with a camera."

Jesse was silent.

"And I realize that I have often been that way with you."

"I know," Jesse said.

"You're not going to help me with this," Jenn said. "Are you?"

"You're doing fine by yourself," Jesse said.

"I'm going to try to be better," Jenn said.

Jesse waited.

"It's a hard balancing," Jenn said. "If I go too far the other way, I give myself away. I become entirely dependent on someone else to direct my likes and dislikes, what I want to do, what I should do. You know?"

"Yes," Jesse said.

"And after a while I resent it, and the resentment builds, and after a while I explode and go the whole other way. Instead of being all about you, it becomes all about me."

"Be nice if you could find a middle ground," Jesse said.

"Yes," Jenn said.

Jesse was lying on his back in the dark, with the phone hunched in his left shoulder. His handgun was on the night table beside the bed. There was no sound in the apartment.

"Maybe I can," Jenn said.

"We both have changes to make," Jesse said.

"I wonder who we'll be when we've made them," Jenn said.

"Whoever we are," Jesse said, "we won't be worse."

"I can't seem to get you out of my life," Jenn said.

"I know," Jesse said.

"Can you wait?" Jenn said. "Until I get better?"

"I have so far," Jesse said.

"But will you still?"

"I don't know, Jenn. I try not to plan too far ahead."

"I don't want a life without you in it."

"That's not entirely up to you, Jenn."

Jenn was quiet for a time. The bedroom was in the back of the apartment, away from the harbor. There was a dim hint of light from the street made a little brighter by the snow cover.

"Is there anyone else?" Jenn said.

"Not yet," Jesse said.

"But there might be?"

"Jenn," Jesse said. "My life would be far less complicated if I could be happy without you."

"I know," she said.

"But so far," Jesse said, "I can't."

They were both quiet, still connected by the phone line, with nothing much else to say. The silence extended.

"The pressure about those serial murders must be awful."

"Everyone feels it would be good to catch them," Jesse said.

"Including you," Jenn said. "That's where the most pressure is."

Jesse didn't comment.

"And you have to carry it alone."

"Not entirely," Jesse said.

"I wish I could help you," Jenn said.

"Be good if you could," Jesse said.

Again they allowed the silence to settle.

"I'm sorry," Jenn said.

"I know."

"I'm working on it," she said.

"I am too."

"I know."

There was more connective silence.

"We'll get there," Jenn said finally.

"We'll get somewhere," Jesse said.

59

When Jesse came into the station house Molly was at the front desk.

"You've reached new heights of popularity," she said.

"Hard to believe," Jesse said

"Tony Lincoln called," Molly said. "He and Mrs. Lincoln will be downtown this morning and would love to buy you lunch."

"I have reached new heights," Jesse said.

"Told you," Molly said.

"They say where?"

"Gray Gull," Molly said. "Twelve-thirty."

"Call them back," Jesse said. "Tell them I'll meet them there."

"What do you suppose they're doing?" Molly said.

"Maybe they'll tell me," Jesse said. "At lunch."

"You might think about being a little careful," Molly said. "Bring some backup maybe?"

"Don't want to discourage them," Jesse said.

"We don't want them discouraging you, either," Molly said. "In a manner of speaking."

"If it comes to confrontation," Jesse said, "I figure I'm better than they are."

"And if you're not?" Molly said.

Jesse shrugged.

"Jesse, you're a good man and a good cop," Molly said. "Better than this town deserves."

"Thank you."

"It matters what happens to you," Molly said.

"The ugly truth of it, Moll, is that it doesn't matter a hell of a lot to me."

Molly looked at him silently. After a time she said, "A lot of people love you, Jesse."

Jesse smiled. "Including you?"

"Especially me," Molly said. "And don't shut me off by being cute."

"It's hard for me not to be cute," Jesse said.

"I give up," Molly said.

They were both silent for a moment.

Then Jesse said, "Thanks, Molly," and went on into his office.

At quarter past twelve Jesse showed up at the Gray Gull, and got a seat by the window, in a corner, where it would be easier to talk. The Lincolns showed up at 12:30. They came in bubbling with good cheer. Tony was wearing a navy pea coat and a gray turtleneck sweater. Brianna had on fur. Jesse didn't know what kind. Jesse stood as they approached.

"Hi," Tony said. "Thanks for coming."

"Never turn down a free lunch," Jesse said.

"Well, I know how busy you must be, but Brianna and I really enjoyed talking to you before, and since we were in the neighborhood."

Jesse nodded. The Lincolns took off their coats and piled them on the empty fourth chair at the table.

"Please," Brianna said. "There's no need for you to stand."

"I'll wait for you," Jesse said.

When they were all seated, the waiter brought menus.

"You come here very much, Jesse?" Brianna said.

"Yes."

"What's good?"

"The view," Jesse said.

Both Lincolns laughed.

"Oh my," Brianna said. "That's not too encouraging."

"I guess we'd best not test the kitchen," Tony said. "Sandwiches okay?"

"Sure," Jesse said.

"It's after noon," Tony said. "Shall we have a cocktail?"

"We really ought to," Brianna said.

Jesse nodded. Both the Lincolns ordered a cosmopolitan. Jesse had cranberry juice and soda.

"Of course," Tony said. "How thoughtless of us. You're on duty."

Jesse let it go.

"The view is certainly everything it should be," Brianna said.

The day was bright, the neck across the harbor was covered with new snow. The ocean water reflected the blue sky.

"It's what they're selling," Tony said. "If Jesse is right about the food."

Jesse ordered the club sandwich again. Tony and Brianna each had tuna salad on toasted whole wheat. *Goes great with the cosmopolitan,* Jesse thought.

"How's the investigation going?" Tony said.

"The serial killings?"

"Yes. Oh, of course," Tony said. "Talk about an amateur. It never occurred to me that you had other cases."

Jesse smiled.

"So in the serial killings," Tony said. "Are you getting anywhere?"

Brianna was silent, listening to her husband, watching Jesse.

"There's progress," Jesse said.

"Really," Tony said. "Are you at liberty to talk about it?"

Jesse shook his head.

"I understand," Tony said.

"I hope none of them suffered," Brianna said.

"The victims?" Jesse shook his head. "It was over pretty quick."

"Good," Brianna said.

"Do you think they knew, before they were shot, that they were going to be shot?"

Jesse shrugged.

"What must it be like," Brianna said. "To know you're going to die."

"Brianna," Tony said. "Everybody knows that."

"It's one thing," Brianna said, "to know you're going to die someday, and quite another to know you're going to die in the next moment."

Tony nodded.

He said, "Have you ever been in that position, Jesse?"

"Facing death?" Brianna said.

Jesse smiled.

"I'm just a small-town cop," Jesse said. "Mostly we give out parking tickets."

He noticed that Brianna had put her hand on her husband's thigh. Neither of them had eaten much of their sandwiches.

"It must make everything very intense," Tony said.

"I always wondered what it was like for the shooter," Jesse said. "That might be intense."

"Exercising the ultimate human power," Tony said.

"If the shooter thinks about that kind of stuff," Jesse said.

"Do you think they do?"

Again Jesse shrugged.

"I'm just a small-town cop," Jesse said. "Mostly we give out parking tickets."

"I read somewhere that you came here from Los Angeles," Tony said.

His wife's hand was still resting on his thigh. He had covered it with his hand as they talked.

"Everybody has to come from someplace," Jesse said.

"I think you are being modest," Brianna said. "I think you might know a lot about being a policeman."

Jesse grinned at them.

"I've got a lot to be modest about," he said.

Tony gestured to the waiter for the check.

"You are a very interesting man," Tony said.

"You certainly are," Brianna said. "I hope you haven't minded us asking you all these dumb questions."

"Not at all," Jesse said. "I wish more citizens were as interested in the police department."

"Well, I don't know why they're not," Tony said.

He stood and put out his hand.

"I know you must be pressed for time."

"A little," Jesse said.

"Go ahead," Tony said. "I've got the check."

"Thanks," Jesse said. "It's been a nice break to talk with you."

"Oh, how nice," Brianna said. "We must do it again soon."

Jesse stood, shook Tony's hand, and Brianna's, and walked to the door. Tony and Brianna watched him go. When he was out of the restaurant they sat back down at the table.

"Can he be as simple as he seems?" Brianna said.

"He probably is," Tony said. "But even if he isn't, what difference does it make. He's simpler than we are."

"You're so sure," Brianna said.

"You can't seriously think that some small-town cop is as smart as we are."

"He didn't say he wasn't from Los Angeles," Brianna said.

"I don't care if he's from Mars," Tony said. "People don't become policemen because they are great thinkers."

"Are we great thinkers," Brianna said.

"We're not ordinary, Brianna. Never forget that we are not ordinary."

She leaned toward him and kissed him on the mouth and let the kiss linger.

"I'll try to remember," she said.

60

Jesse drove up Summer Street with Candace in the front seat beside him.

"I don't even know what a vizsla is," she said.

"It's a Hungarian pointer," Jesse said. "Sort of like a smallish weimaraner, only gold."

"Do they bite?"

"I don't think so," Jesse said. "Are you having second thoughts?"

"No. I want him. I'm just nervous."

"Your parents are okay with this," Jesse said.

"I don't think my mother likes it too much," Candace said. "But my father said yes."

"So it's yes."

"My mother does what Daddy says."

"And why do you want the dog?"

"I want somebody I can love," Candace said.

"Right answer," Jesse said. "But loving isn't enough, you know. You have to take care."

"I know. Feed him. Walk him." She wrinkled her nose. "Clean up after him. I went over all this with my mother and father."

"How is it at home?" Jesse said.

"My mother is kind of, like . . . sulky."

"And your father?"

"Daddy's great."

"Your mother will get over it," Jesse said.

Like I know.

"I never saw Daddy fight with anybody before."

"Like with the Marinos?"

"Yes. He never even gets mad, very much."

Jesse nodded.

"You didn't try to stop it," Candace said.

Jesse smiled. "He was winning," he said.

"You wanted them to get punched up," she said.

"I did."

"Daddy boxed in college, you know."

"I know."

"Did you ever box?"

"I don't box," Jesse said. "I fight."

"What's the difference?"

"Rules," Jesse said. "How is it for you at school."

"Sometimes Bo or Troy will, like, smirk at me when I pass one of them. But they don't say anything. A lot of the kids are great about it. Some of the other boys, football players and stuff, they call me Centerfold."

"Like *Playboy* Centerfold," Jesse said.

She nodded.

"That sucks," Jesse said.

Candace shrugged. Jesse pulled off of Summer Street onto a narrow road that led down to Pynchon Pond.

Bob Valenti lived at the edge of Paradise in a small yellow house that backed up to the pond. The house was right next to the street, and the modest backyard had been enclosed with a wire fence. Jesse pulled his car up in front of the house. He parked without shutting off the engine, so he could leave the heater running.

"There's Goldie," Jesse said.

The vizsla was sitting in the back corner of the yard, motionless, looking through the fence. He saw the car and followed it with his eyes as it parked. He didn't bark.

"Omigod," Candace said. "The poor thing."

"Things will be better for him," Jesse said.

"Yes," Candace said. "I will really take care of him."

"Remember," Jesse said. "He's lost one owner, and is now relocating again."

"I never had a dog before," Candace said.

"Your father said he did."

"Yes."

"He'll be nervous for a while," Jesse said.

"But if I love him . . ."

"He'll get over it," Jesse said.

"I hope my mother isn't mean to him."

"That would be a bad thing," Jesse said. "Can you talk to your father about that?"

Candace nodded.

"Daddy says she won't be mean."

"Your mother probably loves you," Jesse said.

"Of course she does."

"Then we should be able to bring her around if we have to," Jesse said.

"Can I change his name? I hate Goldie for a name."

"Sure, just go slow. Wait until he's used to you."

"I have to think of a new name anyway."

"You might ask your mother to help you think of a new name," Jesse said.

"So she'd feel like he was hers too?"

"Something like that," Jesse said.

They were still for a minute. The heater still on, the motor still running, Candace looking through the car window at the motionless dog.

"It'll be all right?" she said.

"It will," Jesse said. "But you have to give it time."

They sat silently for another moment.

Then Candace said, "Can we get him now?"

"Sure."

They got out of the car and walked through the old unlovely snow toward Valenti's front door. The dog watched them for a moment, and then stood and came down the fence line toward them.

61

Parking on Beacon Hill was impossible in mid summer. In winter, with plowed snow choking the narrow streets, it had become unthinkable. Jesse finally settled for a hydrant on Beacon Street down from the State House, and walked in along Spruce Street, carrying a flowered bottle of Perrier-Jouët.

Rita lived at the Mt. Vernon Street end of Louisburg Square in a high narrow brick townhouse with a dark green door and gold-tipped wrought-iron fencing across the tiny front yard. Jesse rang the bell, and in a moment Rita opened the door.

"Criminal law pays good," Jesse said as he stepped into the dark red foyer.

"Better than working for the Norfolk County DA, which is what I used to do," Rita said.

They went into her living room. There was a fireplace with a fire going. The room was done in a strong yellow with gold drapes striped with dark red. Rita was all in ivory: pants and blouse, and three-inch ivory heels.

"I don't know which is more impressive," Jesse said. "You or the house."

"Me," Rita said and took the champagne bottle from him. "Will you join me in some of this?" she said.

"No. I'll have some club soda, with cranberry juice if you have it."

"I noticed," Rita said. "I also have orange juice."

"I'll start with the cranberry and soda," Jesse said. "If the evening gets really rousing, I'll step up to the OJ."

"I expect it to get rousing," Rita said.

She made Jesse's drink and poured herself some champagne.

"How is my disgusting client doing at his community service?" she said.

"He's there every afternoon after school," Jesse said. "He and Drake treat Feeney like the fink-out that he is, but they're too scared to do anything about it."

"So what are they doing?"

"Make-work mostly. Wash the floors, clean the toilets, polish doorknobs. Molly finds stuff for them."

"They probably ought to get more punishment than that for gang-raping a young girl."

"They had good legal counsel," Jesse said.

Rita smiled.

"You know the argument as well as I do. In order for the justice system to work, every one has the right to the best legal representation they can get."

Jesse nodded.

"Doesn't mean I liked any of them."

"I don't either," Jesse said.

"How's the girl doing?"

Jesse shrugged.

"She and I went out and adopted a dog for her."

"*You* and she?"

"It belonged to one of the serial victims. I was trying to find it a home."

"Did that make her happy."

"I don't think it made her happy. It did give her something to care about."

"What would make her happy?"

"I don't know," Jesse said. "Maybe a couple years with a good shrink."

"Is that going to happen?"

"I gave her a name," Jesse said.

"My goodness," Rita said. "Cop for all seasons."

"I know a shrink," Jesse said.

"You think she'll see the shrink?"

"Most people don't," Jesse said.

Rita nodded.

"I did," she said, "after my last divorce."

"You've had more than one?"

Rita smiled and poured herself more champagne.

"I've had three," she said. "And after each one, I was inclined to fall deeply in love with the next guy I dated."

"You still do that?"

"No," Rita said. "But it doesn't mean I won't."

"After my divorce," Jesse said, "I wanted to fall in love with someone else and couldn't."

"You've only been divorced once?"

"Yes."

"The more it happens, I think," Rita said, "the more desperate you get, and the more likely you are to grab at the first loser that strolls by, which makes it more likely that this marriage will fail, too."

"And you've learned not to do that."

"Until now," Rita said.

Jesse drank. The cranberry and soda seemed particularly insufficient for this moment. They were silent.

Finally, Jesse said, "Me?"

"It feels like it," Rita said.

"Another loser?"

"No," Rita said. "You are not a loser."

"Thank you, but I'm not so sure."

"Because?"

"Because Jenn," Jesse said.

Rita put her glass down and stood, and began to unbutton her blouse. When it was unbuttoned she slid out of it.

She stepped out of her shoes and unzipped her pants, and slid them down over her legs and stepped out of them. Her lingerie was ivory. *So it won't show through,* Jesse thought. She unsnapped her bra, slid out of her underpants, and stood naked in front of him. Jesse smiled.

"A real redhead," he said.

"Or a very thorough colorist," Rita said.

She came to the couch and sat beside Jesse and tucked her feet under her.

"So?" Rita said. "Tell me about Jenn."

"It's a little hard to concentrate," Jesse said.

"My point exactly," Rita said.

She shifted somehow and was in his lap, and then they were both naked, and then, after a while they lay together on the couch with their arms around each other, waiting for their breathing to slow.

Finally, with her face next to his, Rita said, "So, tell me about Jenn."

"You are as good-looking a woman as I have ever met," Jesse said carefully. "And I've never had sex that I liked better."

"Not even Jenn," Rita said.

"She's not better-looking than you are," Jesse said, "and she doesn't make love any better."

"So, why her, not me?"

Jesse eased himself up a little so that his head rested on the arm of the couch. Rita adjusted so that she lay inside his right arm.

"Why her?" Rita said again.

Jesse laughed briefly and without amusement.

"God," he said. "If I knew that, I'd know everything."

"You're sort of an addictive personality," Rita said.

"Booze?" Jesse said.

"And Jenn."

Jesse nodded slowly.

"And Jenn," he said.

"You've stopped drinking," Rita said.

Jesse was silent, listening to his breathing, and Rita's.

"I know," Jesse said.

They lay still, passionless, their naked bodies touching pleasantly. Rita seemed perfectly comfortable without her clothes on.

"Maybe you can break the addiction to Jenn," Rita said.

"I love her," Jesse said.

"Jesus Christ," Rita said. "You invoke that phrase as if you'd discovered the double helix. Love is an emotion, like any other. You can get over it, like you do anger or fear, or hatred."

"I love her," Jesse said. "If I can be with her, I will be."

"So," Rita said, "what's the plan? You fuck me until you can be with her?"

"Hell, Rita, I don't have a plan," Jesse said. "I'm just hanging on."

"That shrink you know," Rita said. "What does he say about Jenn?"

"He says that I do my job, that I have women I care about, who care about me, that my life moves right along, so why do I need Jenn?"

"And your answer?"

"You won't like it," Jesse said.

Rita grimaced.

"'Because I love her'?" Rita said.

Jesse nodded.

"And you don't love me," Rita said.

"Actually I do," Jesse said. "It's just that I love Jenn more."

Rita was quiet for a time.

"If you and Jenn ever get together, why couldn't we love each other, too?" Rita said. "Part-time, so to speak."

"Rita, I don't know what's going to happen after I get off this couch, let alone who I'll be in a month or a year."

"But it might be possible," Rita said.

Jesse shook his head slowly.

"Maybe not," he said.

62

The note was hand printed in big block letters with blue ink.

TO FIND OUT ABOUT YOUR SERIAL
KILLER, BE AT THE FOOD COURT AT
NORTHEAST MALL AT 7 PM. THURSDAY.
ALONE!!!!!!!

The letters looked a little wavery, as if the writer were old.
"Probably printed it left-handed," Jesse said.
"To frustrate the handwriting experts," Molly said.

"Yep."

"Is handwriting analysis really that effective?" Molly said.

Jesse smiled and looked as if he thought it wasn't.

"You know that mall?" Jesse said.

"I'm a suburban mother," Molly said. "Of course I do. Don't you?"

"I'm not a suburban mother," Jesse said. "I'll go up there this afternoon and scope it out."

"You haven't ever been there?"

"Only outside," Jesse said. "When I met Candace there."

"Hard to imagine," Molly said. "Do you think it's them?"

"Yep."

"What are you going to do?"

"Show up," Jesse said.

"It's Tuesday," Molly said. "We have today and tomorrow to get ready."

"How crowded would it be on a Thursday evening," Jesse said.

"Quite," Molly said. "It's crowded every night, and it's time to be buying the spring wardrobe."

"Sure it is."

"There are a bunch of exits from the mall," Molly said. "Not counting the ones that the stores use, you know for truck deliveries and stuff."

"Be hard to cover them all."

"I'm sure the state police will help, and the local cops will give us some people."

Jesse shook his head.

"Too many jurisdictions," he said. "I won't be able to control it."

"We can coordinate through Vargas," Molly said.

"These are smart people," Jesse said.

"But surely they don't think we won't try to catch them," Molly said.

"They probably like that," Jesse said.

"They like it?"

"Raises the risk, makes it more exciting."

"So why not be there in force," Molly said. "Cover every exit, have plainclothes people all over the food court."

"They like risk," Jesse said. "But they don't like certainty. They don't want to get caught. They only want the danger of getting caught."

"They want to be shot at and missed," Molly said.

"Exactly," Jesse said.

"And you're afraid that if there are too many different people involved, somebody will give it away."

"And we'll lose them."

"You're assuming," Molly said, "that their purpose is to kill you."

"Yep."

"So why do it this way. They know where you live. Why not just lurk around there and shoot you when you come home?"

"Same reason they've been flirting with me, buying me lunch, being my pals," Jesse said.

"They are, after all, crazy," Molly said. "I tend to forget that."

"So not everything they do is logical to us," Jesse said. "On the other hand crazy doesn't mean stupid. They've chosen a public place with many exits. The parking lot leads to many roadways that lead in many directions. It is a good place to escape from. It is an easy place not to be noticed. And it is a hard place for us to start shooting."

"So we put our people there, early, around the food court," Molly said. "Suit and I can be there as a married couple shopping for cruise wear."

"You're ten years older than Suit," Jesse said.

"Yes. But I do not look it."

"True," Jesse said. "But it can't be Suit. They know him."

"Well, me and Anthony then," Molly said. "We keep Suit out of sight."

"I don't want it to be you, Moll," Jesse said.

"Why not?"

"You got kids and a husband," Jesse said.

"And Anthony has kids and a wife," Molly said.

"I was afraid you'd remember that," Jesse said.

"It's because I'm a woman," Molly said.

Jesse was silent.

"It is, isn't it," Molly said.

"Yes."

"Well, it's lovely and chivalrous of you," Molly said. "And I know you do it because you care about me. But it still demeans me."

"I know," Jesse said.

"God, you're irritating. I can't even fight with you."

"You and Anthony can be snacking in the food court," Jesse said. "Wear your vest."

"You too," Molly said.

Jesse nodded.

"Spring fashions," he said.

63

They set up early. Molly and Anthony deAngelo, in jeans and winter coats, arrived at 4:30 and began to shop the mall. Molly made several purchases, and Anthony carried her bags and looked bored. They saw no sign of Tony or Brianna Lincoln. Only Jesse and Suitcase Simpson had actually seen the Lincolns. The rest had detailed descriptions. But it was not the same. Outside the mall, Simpson dispersed the other cops, trying to keep all the exits in view. Only Steve Friedman and Buddy Hall were on duty in Paradise.

At 6:27, Molly and Anthony came to the food court. They put their bags down and sat at a table. They looked from where they sat at the various food stands, appeared to reach a decision, and Anthony stood up and went to get them some pork fried rice. The food court was nearly filled. Looking at the customers, Molly realized that several of them could be the Lincolns. At 6:48 Molly decided that she couldn't pretend to eat the rice anymore. She had no appetite, and it was clear that neither did Anthony.

"I'll get us some coffee," she said.

"Cream," Anthony said, "two sugars."

At 6:57 Molly took a cell phone out of her purse and called Simpson outside the mall.

"Hello, honey," she said.

"Molly?"

"Yes. Are you and your brother doing what Nana says?"

"Any sign of action?" Simpson said.

Anthony deAngelo looked like a man whose wife spoke often on the phone, glancing aimlessly around the food court. Molly smiled.

"No, honey, Daddy and I are having coffee, we'll be home in a little while."

"Do you want me to help you with this?" Simpson said. "Pretend I'm your kid?"

"Absolutely not," Molly said. "What have you and Nana been doing?"

"I'll just sort of hum, then, so you'll know the line's open and I'm still here."

"That's very good," Molly said.

At seven o'clock Jesse, wearing a navy pea jacket over his Kevlar vest, walked down the mall with his hands in the pockets and stood in front of the elevator, opposite the entrance to the food court.

"It's seven o'clock," Molly said.

On the phone Suit said, "Jesse there?"

"Un-huh."

"Anything happening?"

"No, honey, not yet."

"I kind of like the *honey* thing. Will you call me honey around the station, after this is over?"

"No."

Behind Jesse the elevator door opened and a man and woman stood in the door. They were wearing hats and scarves that partly hid their faces.

"Jesse," the man said.

As Jesse turned toward them they each raised a long-barreled pistol and shot Jesse in the chest. The pistols made only a flat pop that was lost in the hubbub of the mall. Jesse stepped a half step back.

"It's happening," Molly said into the phone and dropped it and turned with her gun out. DeAngelo was on his feet as well, his handgun leveled.

The elevator door closed and the elevator went back up, taking the man and woman with it. People in the food court area were beginning to react. The result was confusion.

"There's an escalator at each end," Jesse said, pointing. "Molly, cover that one. Anthony, stay here."

Then he turned and ran down the mall, forcing his way through the crowd, his gun held down against his thigh. When he reached the escalator, he slowed and opened his coat so that, as he went up the moving stairs, he could speak into the microphone clipped to his vest.

"Suit?"

"You okay, Jesse?"

"I am. It went down. We've got them somewhere on the second level now."

"Shall we come in."

"No. We'll try to chase them to you."

"We'll be here."

"When we saw them they were wearing black watch caps pulled down over their foreheads, and black or navy scarves wrapped up over their chins, like they were cold. She had on a fur coat. He was wearing a trench coat."

"We'll be looking."

"Make sure everybody gets the message," Jesse said. "And they could change, so don't lock in on the coats and scarves."

"Roger, Jesse."

At the top of the escalator Jesse paused with the gun at his side, looking around. Most people didn't notice the gun. The ones that did looked quickly and moved swiftly away. Jesse made sure his badge, clipped to his vest, was visible. *Don't want somebody calling 911, and end up shooting it out with the local SWAT team.* He looked down to the far end of the mall and saw Molly standing at the top of her escalator.

On the first level, Anthony stood facing the elevator. His gun was in his hand, held down against his right thigh. The elevator came back down and the doors opened and several men and women got out. One of them was a good-looking woman wearing a paisley yellow silk scarf over her head, and an ankle-length yellow wool coat. She carried a small shopping bag, and smiled at Anthony as she headed past him toward the exit. Anthony was pretty sure she wasn't the one. Still, better to play it safe.

"Excuse me, ma'am," Anthony said.

She turned and took the gun from the shopping bag and shot him in the forehead. As Anthony went down, one of the men from the elevator stepped up and took the woman's arm. He was wearing a leather jacket and a long-billed low-crowned baseball hat.

By the time Anthony hit the floor the man and woman were walking firmly past him and out the front door of the mall. As they reached the parking lot several people pushed past them, running toward a Paradise Police car. The people crowded around the car, all talking at once to Eddie Cox and gesturing toward the mall. The man and woman passed the crowd and got into a rented Volvo, and drove quietly away.

64

Jesse sat with Healy in the front seat of Healy's unmarked car.

"We found their other clothes in the washrooms," Healy said.

"Had the change of clothes in the shopping bags," Jesse said.

"Maybe you should have asked for help," Healy said.

"We had all the exits covered," Jesse said.

"Which means they walked right past one of your guys."

"Simpson and I were the only ones really knew what they looked like," Jesse said.

"If you'd brought us in . . ." Healy said.

"You wouldn't have known what they looked like either."

"True, but we might have had more people at the elevator."

"And your people couldn't have started shooting," Jesse said, "any more than Anthony could. There were eight or ten people coming off that elevator."

"And he was probably a little less cautious because it was a good-looking broad," Healy said.

Jesse shrugged.

"Whether it would have gone better if you'd invited us in," Healy said. "It couldn't have gone worse."

"No. One of my guys is dead, and the Lincolns are gone."

"You're sure it was them," Healy said.

"It was them."

"You recognized them."

"It was them."

Healy nodded and didn't speak for a moment.

Then he said, "We're covering their condo. Their Saab is still in their parking lot."

Jesse nodded. "Maybe a rental," he said.

"We'll be checking the rental agencies, but it's," he glanced at the digital clock on his dashboard, "two twenty-six in the morning."

"If they used their own names," Jesse said.

"Have to show a credit card."

"These are people who could have had a whole other identity waiting around in case they needed it," Jesse said.

"Want to go take a look at their home?" Healy said.

"Warrant?" Jesse said.

"Already got that covered," Healy said.

"Why you get the big bucks," Jesse said. "First I have to go see Betty deAngelo."

"The widow?" Healy said.

Jesse nodded.

"Lucky you," Healy said.

"She has five kids," Jesse said.

"Hard," Healy said.

Jesse nodded.

"I'll meet you at the Lincolns' condo," he said.

Jesse got out of the car and walked across the empty parking lot to where his car sat alone near the east entrance of the mall. Behind him Healy's car drove away. Healy was right, Anthony would have hesitated before shooting at a good-looking woman. And Healy was probably right about including the state cops. Jesse should have brought them in. He didn't have enough people. He had more people, maybe it wouldn't have been Anthony. Maybe it wouldn't have been anybody. Maybe they'd have caught the Lincolns. His footsteps were loud in the empty darkness. Maybe he overestimated himself and his men. Maybe thinking about it wasn't useful. He unlocked his car and got in and started it up. The headlights underscored how still and abandoned the parking lot was. He put the car in gear and drove.

He didn't know the names of any of Anthony's children. There was probably an Anthony Junior. He hoped the children wouldn't be there when he had to talk with Betty.

65

When Jesse got to the Lincolns' condominium at 4:15 in the morning, the state crime-scene people were beginning to wind down. A couple of state homicide detectives were poking about.

"Talk to the widow?" Healy said.

Jesse nodded. Healy nodded with him.

"You ever see the den, here?"

"Lot of equipment," Jesse said.

"Take a look," Healy said and walked with Jesse into the den.

On the computer screen was a candid head shot of Jesse

that looked as if it had been taken when he was leaving the Paradise Police Station. The picture had apparently been cropped and blown up so that the background was hard to be sure of.

"We found it on the screen just like this when we came in."

"They thought I'd be dead," Jesse said.

"Yep."

Healy turned and called into the living room.

"Rosario."

One of the crime-scene technicians came into the room.

"Run these pictures through," Healy said.

Rosario looked at the picture on the computer screen, and then at Jesse.

"Captain's afraid of computers," Rosario said.

"I can't even download porn," Healy said. "Run them."

"Yessir, Captain," Rosario said and clicked the mouse.

A picture of Abby Taylor came up. Rosario clicked again. A picture of Garfield Kennedy. Click. Barbara Carey. Click. Kenneth Eisley. Click. Back to Jesse.

"They're all blowups of candid shots," Rosario said. "One of those digital cameras. You plug it into the computer and process it however you want."

"And my picture was on the screen just like that when you came in?"

"Yep."

"Anything else interesting?"

"On the computer?" Rosario said. "Nothing I can find. But maybe the guys in the lab . . ."

"Make sure you don't lose anything," Healy said, "when you shut it down."

Jesse went back to the living room with Healy.

"Anything else interesting?" Jesse said.

"Place is immaculate. No sign of flight. Clothes, toothbrushes, hair spray, all in place. Checkbooks show money in the bank. Couple credit cards in the drawer. Food in the refrigerator. Expiration dates suggest it was bought recently. Concierge doesn't remember them leaving yesterday. But you can take the elevator from their place direct to the lower level, and go out the side door to the parking lot."

"Why are the pictures on the computer screen?" Jesse said.

"I know," Healy said. "It bothers me too."

"It incriminates them," Jesse said.

"Decisively," Healy said.

"So why display them?"

"They didn't expect us to be here?" Healy said.

"Or they did."

Healy walked to the window and looked out. There was nothing to see but himself and the room reflected in the night-darkened glass.

"They wanted us to know?" Healy said.

"Maybe."

Jesse walked over and stood beside Healy, staring at the darkness.

"So how did they know we'd be here?" he said.

"They had no reason to think they wouldn't kill me," Jesse said.

"And if they had killed you," Healy said, "they had no reason to think we'd suspect them."

"But they left what amounts to a confession in plain view," Jesse said.

"To five murders," Healy said. "Or so they expected."

Behind them the specialists were packing up.

"We're about done here, Captain," Rosario said.

Healy nodded. He spoke to one of the detectives.

"Leave a couple of uniforms here," he said. "Case they come back."

"I'll stay a while," Jesse said.

"Sure," Healy said. "You want to be alone?"

"Yeah."

"I like to do that too," Healy said. "Sort of listen to a crime scene. By myself."

"Something like that," Jesse said.

"Okay. Paulie," Healy said to the detective. "Tell the troopers to stay in the vestibule until Stone leaves."

When everyone was gone Jesse stood in the thick silence and looked slowly around the room. The place had been measured, searched, photographed, inventoried, dusted. The computer had been removed. He walked to the bathroom. Two toothbrushes stood in holders. A barely squeezed tube of toothpaste for sensitive teeth lay on the counter. The soap in the soap dish was new. A full bottle of shampoo stood on a shelf in the shower stall beside a fresh bar of soap. On a shelf above the bathroom sink were matched jars and tubes of makeup, all barely used, all in order by size and shape. The bed seemed freshly made. He turned back the spread.

The sheets seemed newly washed and ironed. He opened bureau drawers. Tony's shirts were carefully laid out by color, still in their transparent envelopes from the cleaner. His socks were rolled. Brianna's bureau was equally immaculate. The kitchen was spotless. The counters were washed. The refrigerator was clean and organized. A place for everything and everything in its place. The dining room table was set with good china. The whole place looked as if they were expecting company. . . . They were. That's why they had left the evidence displayed. A farewell. *See how much smarter we are than you are.* They would simply disappear and, in time, someone would notice they were gone, or maybe there would be an anonymous tip. And the cops would come and there would be the confession on the computer screen. They had never planned to come back. And they were too compulsive to leave the place un-immaculate for the company to see. Even had they successfully killed him they were moving on. He was to be the final triumph.

Here.

Jesse talked to the press the next morning on the front steps of the Paradise Police Station. Yes, a Paradise police officer, Anthony deAngelo, had been killed last night. Yes, they had identified two suspects: Tony and Brianna Lincoln. No, they did not know the whereabouts of the suspects. Yes, the search was continuing. When they had asked all the questions Jesse could stand to hear, the news conference ended and Jesse went inside.

Molly nodded toward his office.

"Jenn," Molly said. "She came in the side."

Jesse nodded and walked into his office. Jenn was sitting on the edge of his desk, looking through Jesse's side window at the turmoil of media that surged around the front lawn of the police station. Jesse closed the office door behind him.

"Hi," he said.

"Hi."

Jesse went around the desk and sat in his chair. Jenn shifted on the edge of his desk so she was looking at him, her right leg resting on the ground, her left draped over his desk.

"Are you okay?" she said.

"Physically? Sure," Jesse said. "Small caliber, good vest."

"Still, someone tried to kill you."

"I know."

"And they did kill one of your men."

"Yes."

"And they got away," Jenn said.

"So far," Jesse said.

Jenn was quiet for a moment.

"You must feel awful," she said.

"I try not to feel too much," Jesse said.

"How's the drinking?" Jenn said.

"I don't drink anymore," Jesse said.

Jenn nodded.

"Did you have to tell Anthony's family?"

Jesse nodded.

"His wife," Jesse said.

"Was it bad?"

"Yes."

"And you're sure you don't feel awful?" Jenn said.

Jesse shrugged and looked out the window at the press scrum.

Then he took in some air, and looked back at Jenn and said, "Yes. I guess, in fact, I do."

"Of course you do," she said. "May I say something?"

"If I said no, you'd say it anyway."

Jenn smiled.

"Yes," she said. "I suppose I would."

She paused and pressed her face for a moment into her semi-cupped hands and rubbed her eyes, as if she were very tired. Then she raised her head and took a breath.

"I am very sorry I tried to impose upon our relationship to get a break on this serial killer story," she said. "You didn't need that. You shouldn't have had to address that. I was wrong and stupid to ask."

Jesse smiled faintly.

"Wrong *and* stupid?" he said.

"Yes. I was thinking only about myself. I should have been thinking about you. I'm very sorry."

Jesse said nothing for a time.

Then he said, "Thank you, Jenn."

"You're welcome."

She was wearing perfume. Her hair was well cut and perfectly arranged. Her makeup was bright and expert. Her clothes were very immediate. There was a kind of physical brightness about her that was just short of flamboyant.

"Would you like to talk about it?" she said.

"Off the record?"

Jenn hung her head a little.

"I'll never tell anyone," she said, "what you say to me unless you ask me to."

Jesse smiled at her.

"Besides," he said. "You don't even have B-roll for this."

Jenn smiled back at him.

"Hell," she said. "All there is in this case, is B-roll."

"There's two of them, husband and wife. Their goal was to kill me, but I was wearing a vest. We tried to trap them at the shopping center but they killed Anthony and got away in the crowd. Probably should have brought the state cops into it, but coulda, shoulda. We searched their condo, found a computer with my picture on it and, in the sequence of their deaths, the other victims."

"Like a confession," Jenn said.

"Seemed so. The apartment was empty. No sign of flight, but no sign of them returning either. Their car is still in the garage. They probably had a rental. Staties are checking that now. My guess is that these people have already prepared another identity and the Staties won't find anybody named Lincoln renting a car."

"So you think you were going to be the *pièce de résistance*?" Jenn said.

"Yes."

"And they planned to disappear after they shot you?"

"Yes. The house is anally cleaned for us. The pictures on the computer are waiting for us to find them. See how much smarter we are than you shitkickers."

"And you don't know where they went," Jenn said.

"No idea."

"How did they get to the car?"

Jesse stared at her.

"They had to pick up the rental car," Jenn said. "How did they get there?"

"How did they get the car," Jesse said.

67

"Maybe one of them drove the other one over," Simpson said. "To get the rental car."

"Did they stash the rental at their condo?" Jesse said. "After they picked it up?"

"Where?" Simpson said. "All the parking spaces are assigned. If they put it in somebody else's spot it would draw attention."

"Which they don't want to do," Jesse said. "Maybe on the street?"

"It's a tow zone on both sides of the road," Simpson said. "Side road."

"In theory," Simpson said, "that's resident parking only."

"How often do we enforce that?"

"Not often," Simpson said.

"But they don't know that," Jesse said.

"So anything they did with the rental car would risk drawing attention, which, obviously, they needed to avoid."

"Or they parked it at the mall, earlier in the day," Jesse said. "And took cabs."

Simpson said, "You think they're dumb enough to take a cab?"

"They think they are brilliant," Jesse said. "And they think we're stupid."

"So they could have."

"Yes."

"Paradise Taxi is the only one in town," Simpson said.

"Go see them," Jesse said.

"Now?"

"Now."

When Suit was gone, Jesse swung his chair around and put his feet up on the sill of his back window and looked out at the fire trucks parked in front of the fire station. The phone rang. Jesse answered.

"Captain Healy," Molly said, "on line two."

"Bullets match," Healy said.

"The one they took out of Anthony?"

"Yep. And the ones that were trapped in your vest."

"We knew they would," Jesse said. "How about the car rental companies."

"The rental companies are an air ball," Healy said. "We

checked in a fifty-mile radius, including Logan Airport. Nobody named Lincoln rented a car."

"How about the ones that deliver?"

"You thought of that, too," Healy said.

"We're a small department," Jesse said. "But we try hard."

"There's only two companies in the fifty-mile radius that deliver," Healy said. "Neither one of them has delivered to Paradise."

"You get any print matches from their condo?" Jesse said.

"Nope. They're not in the system that we can find. You know it's not really their condo?"

"They rent it?"

"Yep, from a guy working a two-year consulting project in Saudi Arabia."

"He'll be pleased to hear they took off," Jesse said.

"Unless they paid up front."

"Would you?" Jesse said.

"When I knew I was going to disappear? No, I don't think I would."

When he was off the phone Jesse swiveled his chair, put his feet back on the windowsill, and looked at the fire trucks again.

They had a false identity. They must have had it in place, standing by. That's why they had been so easy and open about their history in Cleveland. Maybe the Cleveland identity was assumed too. If you had time and some smarts you could prepare a full new one, driver's license, credit cards. Or five full new ones.

Standing on the running board of one of the fire trucks, a

news photographer was taking pictures through the window. Jesse could imagine the caption. *Paradise Police Chief Jesse Stone ponders his next move.* Jesse kept sitting.

If they had a long-established alternate identification, then they must have had a long-established plan to kill people. Maybe Paradise wasn't the first. People like that didn't stop very often. If Paradise wasn't the first place they'd pursued their passion, it probably wouldn't be the last. They were unconnected. They didn't need to work.

Suitcase Simpson came into the office.

"There were eleven cab fares in the last week," Suit said, "out of Paradise. Seven of them went to the airport. Two went to the Northeast Mall. One went to New England Baptist Hospital. One went to Wonderland Dog Track."

"In the winter?" Jesse said.

"They run all year," Suit said.

"In this weather it would be easier just to mail them a check," Jesse said.

"You California guys are wimps," Suit said. "Hardy New Englanders like to be there when they lose it."

Jesse nodded.

"So they could have cabbed to the airport, picked up the rental, drove it to the mall."

"Or one of them could have, and the other one could have picked him up and driven him home in the Saab."

"They like to do things together," Jesse said.

"So you figure they both went for the rental car, and drove it to the mall in time for the shootout?"

"Yes."

"What if they rented it the day before," Suit said, "and parked it at the mall?"

"The car would have been parked there overnight. It might have attracted attention. And they'd have had to take a cab to the mall on the day of the shooting."

"Why wouldn't they have just driven the Saab over and left it when they swapped cars?"

"Don't know. Maybe they're so yuppied out that they couldn't bear to abandon the Saab."

"Hell, Jesse, they abandoned it anyway, along with their condo."

"Yeah, but it was safely parked in the garage. We are not dealing with entirely rational people here."

"You think they're crazy?"

"They've killed a bunch of people for no apparent reason."

"Good point," Suit said. "Either way we're looking for cab rides on the day of the shooting."

Jesse said, "Isn't there a subway station near the dog track?"

"Yeah. On the Blue Line. We used to take it into Boston when I was a kid. Buncha stops: Revere Beach, Orient Heights, the airport, Maverick Square in East Boston."

Jesse nodded.

"Okay," he said. "Check the cabs to the airport and to Wonderland on that day. Talk to the drivers. See if they can describe who they took, and where they picked them up. Get a list of names from all the rental companies at the airport, who they rented a car to that day."

"That's going to take some time," Suit said.

"It might," Jesse said. "Or you might score the first guy you ask."

"Not likely," Suit said.

"Just as likely as last," Jesse said.

"No," Suit said. "It never happens like that."

Jesse shrugged.

When Suit was gone, Jesse looked at the fire engines some more.

So, where would they go? They were free to go anywhere. They clearly had plenty of money. Tony's ocular scanner made that possible. If it were true. . . . Maybe it was. . . . If it were true, he'd hold a patent on it. . . . If he held a patent on it, they'd have it at the U.S. Patent Office . . . which would have a website.

Jesse stood and opened his office door and yelled, "Molly."

When she came in, he said, "Are you as expert on the Internet as you are at everything else?"

"You sound like my husband," Molly said, "when he wants something."

"I need crime fighting help," Jesse said.

"You really don't want to do this yourself," Molly said. "Do you."

"I need you to find the U.S. Patent Office on the Web and see who has patented an optical scanning device."

"Everybody?"

The Lincolns appeared to be in their late forties.

"Everybody in, oh, say, the last twenty-five years."

"And while I'm doing that," Molly said, "you'll be in here oiling your baseball glove? Thinking of spring?"

"Hey," Jesse said, "I'm the chief of police."

Molly smiled and saluted.

"Of course you are," she said. "I'll see what I can find."

68

Jesse sat with **Marcy Campbell** in the Indigo Apple drinking coffee.

"Rita Fiore never called me back," he said.

"Maybe she's decided she won't waste any more time with you."

"Even though I'm a sexual athlete?"

"It sounds like Rita wants, excuse the phrase, *a relationship*," Marcy said.

"And she's thinks I'm not a good candidate?"

"You're not," Marcy said.

"I know."

"And she knows."

Jesse nodded.

"She wants a husband," Jesse said.

"Or the equivalent," Marcy said.

"I think she's had several of those already."

"Give her credit," Marcy said, "for fierce optimism."

"There are women who need a mate, I guess."

"People," Marcy said.

"People?"

"Men *and* women," Marcy said, "who feel incomplete unless they are mated."

"You're not one of them," Jesse said.

"No. I like sex and I like companionship, but not at the expense of my freedom or my self."

Jesse broke off a small piece of orange cranberry muffin and ate it. When he had swallowed, he said, "Maybe I'm one of them."

"Well," Marcy said. "You're an odd case. You're like me, except for Jenn. You like sex and companionship, too. But you won't commit to a new relationship just to have it. It's why we get along so well, neither of us requires commitment from the other."

Jesse laughed. "Which produces," he said, "a kind of commitment to each other."

"I suppose so," Marcy said. "But not for the same reasons. I am true to myself. You are true to Jenn."

"Which may be a way of being true to myself."

Marcy nodded.

"Or maybe obsessive."

"There's that," Jesse said.

Marcy sipped her coffee, holding the mug in both hands.

"But goddamnit," she said, "I'll give you credit, you are true to it, whatever the hell it is."

"Well, the thing is," Jesse said. "I love her."

"That simple," Marcy said.

Jesse nodded.

"Is there anything Jenn could do that would make you give her up?" Marcy said.

"She could tell me that she had no further interest in me," Jesse said. "If she told me that I'd move on."

"Which gives her control," Marcy said.

"I suppose."

"That doesn't bother you?"

"I don't care about stuff like that," Jesse said. "I love her. We're still connected. I'll play it out."

Marcy drank some coffee, and looked at Jesse for a while, and shook her head slowly. Jesse watched her.

"You have given over the crucial decision of your life to someone else," Marcy said. "And what's so odd is that it seems to be evidence of your autonomy."

"Autonomy," Jesse said.

"Don't be cute. You know what it means."

"Sort of."

"You feel strongly. You trust what you feel. And you proceed with it."

"True," Jesse said.

"It's the same in your work. You know what you know, and you do what you do and you plow along doing it."

"Like a mule," Jesse said.

"Or a jackass."

Jesse smiled.

"Same thing," he said. "More or less."

"If you ever work it out with Jenn, will we still be pals?"

"Sure," Jesse said.

"And fuck buddies?"

Jesse breathed slowly in and slowly out. He looked at Marcy for a moment. Then he smiled slightly and shook his head.

"Probably not," he said.

69

Suit and Molly sat at the long table in the conference room. They were drinking coffee from paper cups. A third cup, with the plastic lid still on it, sat at the head of the table. A box of Dunkin' Donuts was open on the table. Suit had his notebook open in front of him. Molly had a computer printout. Jesse came in, examined the box of donuts for a moment, took one, and sat at the head of the table and took the lid off the coffee. He took a bite of the donut.

"Cinnamon," he said.

"I know you like them," Molly said.

"What're the ones with no hole and chocolate frosting?"

"Boston cream," Molly said.

"Good God," Jesse said. "What have you got, Suit?"

"Okay," Suit said. He looked at his open notebook.

"First thing. Nobody took a cab to the mall on the day of the shooting. The two cab rides to the mall were two days earlier and are regulars. Two sisters who live together and go shopping every week."

"Okay," Jesse said. "Anyone picked up at the Lincolns' condo on the day of the shooting?"

"No. But the cab company has a log, you know for taxes and shit. There was a fare went from Paradise to Wonderland on the day of the shooting. I know the cabdriver. Mackie Ward, we played football in high school. Mackie says he picked up a couple who fit our description, down in front of the Chinese restaurant on Atlantic Ave., in the morning on the day of the shooting, and took them to Wonderland."

"They hail him?"

"No. They called for a cab and asked to be picked up there."

"Probably a cell phone," Jesse said. "Okay. So they take the cab to Wonderland. They take the train to Logan. Take the bus to one of the terminals. Catch the rental car bus in front of the terminal and go and pick up the rental car."

"Pretty elaborate," Molly said. "They knew if they killed a cop we'd look for them hard."

"Too elaborate. It's what amateurs do. They would have been much better off to drive the Saab to the airport, park it at the airport parking garage, pick up the rental car, and drive to the mall. You got anything else?"

"There were two other cab fares to the airport the day of the shooting," Suit said. "Both guys, alone."

"We'll check everything," Jesse said. "But it'll turn out to be Wonderland. How'd you make out, Moll?"

Molly finished chewing some donut, and sipped a little coffee.

"Piece of cake," she said. "There are thirteen hundred and twenty-three listings for ocular scanning devices on the Patent Office website."

"Names?" Jesse said.

"Yes, and cities."

"Where they live or where they did the invention?"

"Don't know."

"Anybody named Lincoln?"

"No."

"Anybody from Cleveland."

"Didn't check by city, yet."

"Okay."

Jesse looked at the donuts.

"Boston cream?" he said to Molly.

"You know, like Boston cream pie, except it's a donut."

"And Boston cream pie is a cake, isn't it?"

"Technically."

Jesse took a Boston cream donut from the box and put it on a napkin in front of him and looked at it.

"I bet it would be easy to get this all over you," he said.

"Easier than you can imagine," Molly said. "It may be that only women can eat them."

"The neater species," Jesse said.

"Exactly."

They were quiet while Jesse took a careful bite of the donut. He chewed and swallowed and nodded slowly.

"Good body," Jesse said, "with a hint of insouciance."

"Insouciance?" Suit said.

"I don't know what it means either," Jesse said. "Suit, you get hold of Healy. Tell him we need the names of everybody who rented a car the day of the shooting. He'll have a list. They've already told me there's no one named Lincoln."

"And I'll see how many ocular scanners are listed from Cleveland," Molly said. "It might narrow the cross-referencing."

"Don't bother," Jesse said. "We'll have to check every name against the list of car rentals, anyway. They might not have patented it from Cleveland, or in Cleveland, or whatever the hell one does to get Cleveland mentioned."

"And when we're done?" Suit said.

"If we get a match we might have their new identity."

70

Before he went to work, Jesse drove out to the Neck to see Candace and the dog. It was early March and still wintry with the ugly snow compacting where the plows had spilled it. The sky was overcast. As he drove across the causeway, the ocean, off to his right, was a sullen gray, with a few seabirds wheeling above it. When he got out of his car at the top of Candace's long curved driveway he could smell the approaching snow. It hadn't taken him long, when he'd come from Los Angeles, to learn the anticipatory smell of it.

There were cars in the driveway when Jesse arrived, so he parked on the street and walked up. A sign hanging from the knob on the front door read OPEN HOUSE. BROKERS

ONLY. PLEASE COME IN. Below the invitation was a small logo with a house in it, and the words "Pell Real Estate." Jesse went in. A woman sat on a folding chair at a card table in the hall. She had a pile of brochures on the table in front of her, and a guest book. Jesse could hear voices and movement elsewhere in the house. The sound had the kind of echoed quality that one gets in a house devoid of furniture or rugs.

"Hi," the woman said, "here for the open house?"

"I'm here to see Candace Pennington," Jesse said.

"You're not a broker?"

"No."

"I'm sorry, the Penningtons have moved."

"When?"

"Last week."

"Do you know where they went?"

"I don't really know," the woman said. "I'm just supervising the open house."

She was a heavy exuberant woman with short hair colored very blond.

"Who would know?"

"Oh, I'm sure the office has their new address," the woman said. "You could check with Henry."

"Henry?"

"Henry Pell. Are you interested in the house?"

In the rooms that Jesse could see, the furniture was gone. There were no rugs or drapes. The house was blank, waiting to be re-created.

"No," Jesse said, "I'm not."

As he walked back down the curving drive toward the street, the snow had begun, a few flakes drifting down. More would follow, he knew. They were saying three to six inches. Weather Girl Jenn would be breaking into the regular programming with weather updates from Storm Center 3. Maybe standing in the parking lot. With her designer wool watch cap pulled down just right over her ears. And the flakes fluttering past. As Jesse drove back across the causeway, the snow came straight in at the windshield. Small flakes, the kind all the old-time townies said meant a heavy snowfall. He wasn't long enough out of Southern California to argue the point, though in the time he'd been here he'd seen no correlation.

He could call Henry Pell and get Candace's new address. He wasn't sure he would. They'd taken her where they needed to take her. Where she had no history. Where there were no stories about her. No giggles in the hallways. No covert gestures about sex. No fears that a naked picture of her might surface. What did he have to say to her about that? What did anybody?

The snow had begun to accumulate and the roads were becoming slick as Jesse parked in his spot by the police station, and went in. Bo Marino was mopping the floor in the area of the front desk. Jesse went past him to his office and stopped in the doorway and looked back.

"Where are the other two?" Jesse said.

"Cleaning the cells," Molly said.

Jesse nodded and continued to look at Marino. Was it possible that a jerk like this kid could grow into a decent man? Would the rape follow him and the other two, the way it was following Candace? Marino realized Jesse was looking at him.

"What?" he said.

Jesse didn't answer.

"What are you looking at me for?" Marino said.

Jesse didn't seem to hear him.

You could protect, Jesse thought, and you could serve. But you couldn't really save.

Marino looked at Molly.

"How come he's staring at me like that?" he said.

"Just get the floor clean," Molly said.

At least keep the floor clean, Jesse thought. He went into his office and closed the door. *Better than nothing.*

71

Molly and Suit came into Jesse's office together. They looked pleased with themselves.

"The seven hundred and twenty-eighth name on the patent list is Arlington Lamont," Molly said. "The patent was filed from San Mateo, California, wherever that is."

"Up by San Francisco," Jesse said. He sat motionless with the palms of his hands pressed together in front of him, his chin resting on the fingertips.

"And," Suit said, "on the day of the murder, Arlington Lamont rented a Volvo Cross Country Wagon from Hertz at the airport."

With the palms still pressed, Jesse lowered his hands and

pointed his fingers at Suit and dropped his thumbs like the hammer on a gun.

"Bada bing," he said.

They were all quiet.

"So maybe Lincoln is the phony ID," Jesse said. "And Lamont is the real one."

"Same initials," Molly said. "Anthony Lincoln, Arlington Lamont."

Jesse nodded.

"Hertz requires driver's license and credit card," Jesse said.

"Mass driver's license," Suit said. "American Express card."

"How long?" Jesse said.

"They rented it to him for a week."

"Returning it where?"

"Toronto airport," Suit said. "You think they're actually going to return it?"

"Attract less attention than if they dumped it," Jesse said. "They don't expect us to have their name."

"The credit card number will help us track them," Molly said. "You want me to hop on the phone and see what I can do?"

"No," Jesse said. "I'll let Healy do that. They've got more resources and more clout than we have."

"You think they're going to settle in Canada?"

"Maybe, or maybe it's just a big city with a big airport. Molly, find out how many airlines fly out of Toronto and call all of them and see if any of them have reservations for Mr. and Mrs. Arlington Lamont."

"Every airline?" Molly said. "That's a lot of time to be on hold."

"And keep checking with Hertz," Jesse said. "To see if the car got returned anywhere."

"We could ask them to call us when the car showed up."

Jesse looked at her without speaking.

"Or not," Molly said.

"Call them every day," Jesse said. "Give you something to do while you're on hold with the airlines."

"If I time it right," Molly said, "I can be on hold with both at the same time."

"Lucky we have two lines," Jesse said. "Suit, you call the San Mateo cops, see if you can find anything at all about Mr. or Mrs. Arlington Lamont. If they can't give you anything try San Francisco."

"While we're doing all this phoning," Suit said, "what are you going to do?"

"I have several donuts to eat," Jesse said.

72

"How's the drinking?" Dix said.

"I haven't had a drink in three weeks and four days," Jesse said.

Dix smiled. "And there are several minutes every day when you don't miss it."

"Not that many," Jesse said.

"And you recently escaped death," Dix said.

"I did. Anthony deAngelo didn't."

"How do you feel about that?"

"I should have had more cops on the scene," Jesse said.

"Tell me about that," Dix said.

"I could have had state police support. I chose not to. I wanted to do it ourselves."

"Because they had done their crimes in your town?"

"Because they had killed Abby Taylor."

Dix nodded.

"I took it personally," Jesse said.

"You're a person," Dix said.

"Meaning?"

"Meaning it is impossible not to take things, at some level, personally."

"So what about professional?" Jesse said.

"Things exist simultaneously," Dix said.

"Meaning I can take it personally and be professional?"

"Meaning you need to be two contradictory things at the same time."

Jesse sat quietly.

Then he said, "You know about that."

"Of course."

"It's what you have to deal with."

"What do you think all the rigmarole of psychotherapy is about."

"You have to care about your patient," Jesse said. "But you can't let the caring interfere with your treatment."

Dix made a movement with his head that might have been a nod. Jesse was quiet again.

"You know the kid that got raped?" he said after a while.

Dix did the head movement again.

"She's gone. The family put the house up for sale and moved away."

"Do you know why they moved?" Dix said.

"I assume it was too tough on her in school. You know what kids are like."

Dix smiled faintly and waited.

"I couldn't save her," Jesse said.

"Why would you think you could? You did what you are able to do. You caught her rapists and brought them to justice."

"Yeah. A few months swabbing floors after school in the police station."

"That's the justice that was available," Dix said. "You couldn't prevent her rape. You can't prevent her peers from alluding to it."

Jesse looked past Dix out the window. It was a fresh bright day, intensified by the new snow.

"It seems to me that nobody can protect anybody."

"Risk can be reduced," Dix said.

"But not eliminated."

Dix was quiet, waiting. Jesse said nothing, still looking out the window.

"There's a point," Dix said after a while, "where security and freedom begin to clash."

At midday the sun was strong enough to melt the snow where it lay on dark surfaces. The tree limbs had begun to drip. Jesse turned his gaze back onto Dix.

"You're not just talking about police work," Jesse said.

Dix tilted his head a little and said nothing. *The rigmarole of psychotherapy.*

"People need to live the life they want to live," Jesse said. "They can't live it the way somebody else wants them to."

Dix smiled and raised his eyebrows.

"Everybody knows that," Jesse said.

Dix nodded.

"And few people actually believe it," Jesse said.

"There's often a gap between what we know and what we do," Dix said.

"Let me write that down," Jesse said.

"Psychotherapy is not snake dancing," Dix said. "Mainly it's just trying to close the gap."

Jesse's lungs seemed to expand and take in deeper breaths of air.

"Jenn," he said.

Dix looked noncommittal.

73

When Jesse came into the station Molly was making coffee.

"Hertz says the Volvo got turned in at the Toronto airport," she said.

"Nice to know we can trust them," Jesse said.

Molly poured water into the green Mr. Coffee machine.

"And," Molly said, "nobody who flies out of Toronto has any reservations for Arlington Lamont."

"They could just show up and buy a ticket."

"Doesn't seem like their style," Molly said. "They reserved the rental ahead of time. They think they're safe."

"Did they rent another car?"

"Not from Hertz," Molly said.

"Call the other rental companies and check," Jesse said.

"Soon as I make us coffee," Molly said.

She spooned ground coffee into the filter.

"I will also expect the department to pay all medical bills related to getting concrete information in a human voice from twenty-three airlines," Molly said.

Jesse nodded.

"Beyond the call of duty," Jesse said. "I'm sure we can do something for you."

"Suit's in a car today, seven to three, but he says tell you that he's talked with San Mateo and the only thing they could tell him was that, according to the 1993 telephone directory, Arlington Lamont lived there. And by 1996 he didn't."

"Any unsolved homicides?" Jesse said.

"Suit asked them that. They said they'd get back to him."

"He talk to San Francisco?"

"Yes. They have nothing."

"Do me one other favor?" he said.

"Maybe," Molly said.

"Let me know when the coffee's done," Jesse said.

"Better than that," Molly said. "I'll bring you some."

"Thank you," Jesse said.

"I'm sucking up to you," Molly said. "'Cause you're the chief."

"Good a reason as any," Jesse said and went into his office.

He sat at his desk and put his feet up and looked out the window at the relentless cluster of media. It was about a ten-hour drive to Toronto if you went out the thruway and crossed near Buffalo. They could have gone up 81 through Watertown, about the same distance. He'd check with customs. But the border was an easy one, and an attractive couple driving a Volvo wagon wasn't too likely to be questioned. There were 2.3 million people in Toronto. It wasn't exactly like having them cornered. Jesse tapped the desktop with his fingertips. Molly came in with two cups of coffee.

"Two?" Jesse said.

"One for you," she said. "One for Captain Healy."

Jesse glanced past Molly toward the doorway.

"I saw him parking outside," Molly said. "I figured he wasn't coming to see me."

She put one cup down in front of Jesse, and one cup on the edge of the desk near the guest chair, and went back to the front desk. In about thirty seconds Healy came in.

Jesse pointed at the second cup.

"Coffee," he said.

Healy hung his coat on a rack in the corner, sat down, and picked up the coffee.

"You run a hell of a department," he said.

Jesse nodded. They both sipped some coffee. When he had swallowed and put his cup down, Healy said, "Mr. and Mrs. Arlington Lamont reserved a room at the Four Seasons Hotel in Toronto and guaranteed it with their American Express card."

"They check in?"

"Yep."

"They there now?" Jesse said.

"Nope," Healy said.

He grinned.

"Toronto cops went there a half hour ago and picked them up," he said.

Jesse had the same feeling he'd had with Dix. His chest expanded. He pulled in a large amount of clean air. He exhaled slowly through his nose. Then he reached across the desk and put his clenched fist out toward Healy. Healy tapped it with his own.

"I think I'll go up," Jesse said. "See how they're doing."

74

Mr. and Mrs. Lamont were being held at Division 52 on the west end of Dundas Street, near the lake. Jesse stood outside an interview room with a sergeant of detectives named Gordon. There was a one-way glass window. Behind it Jesse could see the Lamonts sitting at one side of a table, holding hands. There was a uniformed Toronto policeman with them, leaning on the wall.

"They give you any trouble when you picked them up?" Jesse said.

"Nope. Peaceful and innocent," Gordon said. *"Officer, there must be some mistake."*

"They killed five people in my town," Jesse said.

"Lotta pressure on you," Gordon said.

"One of them was a woman I went out with."

"*Lotta* pressure," Gordon said.

"Find any weapons?"

"Two twenty-two long target pistols," Gordon said. "Unloaded and disassembled and packed away in their luggage. You been looking for those?"

"I have."

They stood silently looking through the window at the man and woman holding hands.

"I'll talk to them alone," Jesse said. "Though it's possible that the man may assault me and I'll have to defend myself."

Gordon was a short thick bald man with enough stomach to make the buttons pull a little on his shirt. He nodded thoughtfully.

"You got a right to defend yourself," he said.

Jesse nodded. Gordon unlocked the door and went in and nodded his head to the uniform to leave.

"A visitor," he said to the man and woman.

Jesse came into the interview room. Gordon went out and closed the door behind him. Jesse stood and looked at them.

"Jesse," the man said.

"We're so glad to see you," the woman said.

Jesse didn't say anything. He stood motionless on the other side of the table, looking down at them.

"Jesse," the man said, "what's going on? They didn't even

tell us why they arrested us, just that we were wanted in the States."

Jesse looked straight down at them and didn't say anything.

"Wanted for what?" the man said.

"Jesse, what is it?" the woman said.

Jesse gestured with one hand at the man to stand up. When the man was standing Jesse called him closer with his crooked forefinger. The man was compliant. He walked closer. Jesse put up both hands to tell him to stop, then Jesse stepped in closer to him and drove his knee into the man's groin. The man screamed and staggered backward, bent over, and fell on the floor. He brought his knees to his chest and lay with his hands between his legs and moaned. The woman jumped up and ran around the table toward him and Jesse hit her, a full swing, across the face, with the flat of his open hand. She staggered backward and bumped the wall and slid down and sat hard on the floor, with her face pressed into her hands, and began to cry. Jesse looked at both of them for a moment and then turned and looked at the opaque one-way window and jerked his thumb toward the door. In a moment Gordon came in.

"Lucky to escape with your life," Gordon said. "Eh?"

75

It was snowing softly. Jesse had parked his Explorer at
the town beach, and he and Jenn sat in the front seat looking at the ocean through the clear quarter circle made on
the windshield by the sweep of the wipers. A hundred yards
out the snow and the ocean became indistinct. There was no
one else in the parking lot, no one on the beach. Jesse could
feel how isolated the car would look from a far distance,
alone in the snow at the edge of the sea.

"You all right?" Jenn said.

"Yes."

"You'd say that even if you weren't," Jenn said.

"I know."

"This has been an especially difficult time for you."

"It's why I get the big bucks," Jesse said.

Behind them a plow clattered across the causeway toward Paradise Neck. When it had passed, the silence was broken only by the sound of the wipers and the low fan sound of the heater.

"Did they tell you why they did it?" Jenn asked.

"No."

"Did you ask?"

"No."

Jenn put her hand out, and Jesse took it. Holding hands, they looked silently at the snow and the ocean.

"I have not really been happy," Jenn said, "since the first time I cheated on you."

Jesse didn't say anything. He looked straight ahead at the snow and the water.

"You haven't either," Jenn said.

Jesse nodded. The snow was falling faster. It was harder to see the ocean. He could hear Jenn take a deep breath.

"I think we should try again," she said.

Jesse didn't look at her. The sentence hung in the silence.

"Why," he said after a time, "would it work better this time?"

"We want it to," Jenn said. "We've changed. We're older. We've had some therapy. We know that no one else will quite do."

Jesse was silent.

"We could be on a trial basis." Jenn was talking faster now. "You know? Like a trial separation, only the reverse."

Jesse's throat felt thick. He cleared it.

"How would this work?" Jesse said.

"We wouldn't have to even live together. In fact it might work better if we didn't. We'd keep doing what we do, and see each other on weekends, maybe some night during the week, you know, like a date."

The lady or the tiger, Jesse thought.

"We wouldn't have to get married again, or at least not right away, we could see how this worked."

She held his hand tightly.

"I need to get out of the car," Jesse said.

Jenn nodded and let go of his hand and they got out. They walked together through the snow to the little roofed pavilion at the edge of the beach. In its shelter they stood together, holding each other's hand again. There wasn't much wind and it wasn't very cold. All around the pavilion the snow fell straight down. The smell of the ocean was strong.

"We love each other, Jesse."

Jesse nodded.

"I was learning to be without you," he said.

"We love each other."

Jesse nodded again. Jenn put her head against his shoulder. The only sound was the movement of the water. He cleared his throat again.

"I met a lot of women I liked," Jesse said.

Jenn kept her head against his shoulder. The beach was snow-covered except at the margin where the waves rolled in and out, washing the snow.

"What about that?" Jesse said.

Jenn shook her head slowly against his shoulder.

"No other people?" Jesse said.

"Monogamous," Jenn said softly.

Still holding her hand, Jesse turned toward her. She pressed her face against his neck.

"The magic word," he said.

"I know."

"The one condition," Jesse said.

"Yes."

He continued to hold her hand with his. He put his free arm around her shoulders. Under the sea smell, her perfume was gently determined.

"Okay," Jesse said. "Let's give it another try."